DON'T CHECK OUT THIS BOOK!

DON'T CHECK OUT THIS BOOK!

Kate Klise

illustrated by

M. Sarah Klise

Algonquin Young Readers

2021

Published by
Algonquin Young Readers
an imprint of Algonquin Books of Chapel Hill
Post Office Box 2225
Chapel Hill, North Carolina 27515-2225

a division of
Workman Publishing
225 Varick Street
New York, New York 10014

First Algonquin paperback edition, Algonquin Young Readers, August 2021.
Originally published in hardcover by Algonquin Young Readers in March 2020.
Printed in the United States of America.
Published simultaneously in Canada
by Thomas Allen & Son Limited.
Design by M. Sarah Klise.

LIBRARY OF CONGRESS CATALOGING-IN-PUBLICATION DATA
Names: Klise, Kate, author. | Klise, M. Sarah, illustrator.
Title: Don't check out this book! / Kate Klise ; illustrated by M. Sarah Klise.
Other titles: Do not check out this book!
Description: Chapel Hill, North Carolina : Algonquin Young Readers, 2020.
| Audience: Ages 8-12. | Audience: Grades 4-6. |
Summary: When Appleton Elementary's new school board president,
Ivana Beprawpa, uses her position to line her own pockets, student sleuths Sarah
and May, supported by passionate librarian Rita B. Danjerous, seek the truth.
Told through letters, memos, and text messages.
Identifiers: LCCN 2019037865 | ISBN 9781616209766 (hardcover)
| ISBN 9781643750583 (ebook)
Subjects: CYAC: Schools—Fiction. | Conduct of life—Fiction.
| Books and Reading—Fiction. | Investigative reporting—Fiction. | Letters—Fiction.
Classification: LCC PZ7.K684 Don 2020 | DDC [Fic]—dc23
LC record available at https://lccn.loc.gov/2019037865

ISBN 978-1-64375-190-0 (PB)

10 9 8 7 6 5 4 3 2 1
First Paperback Edition

This book is dedicated to the rabble-rousing librarians
and scandal-stomping young readers
in whom we place
our last, best hope for democracy.

DON'T CHECK OUT THIS BOOK!

DON'T
CHECK
OUT
THIS
BOOK!

Ripeness is all.

—William Shakespeare, *King Lear*

To: Noah Memree

From: Gladys Friday

Subject: New librarian

Date: August 14

Dear Mr. Memree,

The new librarian called this morning. She's arriving on Monday and wants to know if there's space in the library for a few of her favorite books.

Also, she has a daughter (age 10) and is wondering if we have room for her in the fifth-grade class.

Hope you enjoyed your summer vacation!

Gladys Friday
Gladys Friday
Appleton Elementary School Secretary

APPLETON ELEMENTARY SCHOOL
314 Apple Pie Avenue ⊙ Appleton, Illinois 61428
**"We aim to grow with excellence and avoid
branching out unless absolutely necessary"**

To: Gladys Friday

From: Noah Memree

Subject: RE: New librarian

Date: August 14

Ms. Friday:

New librarian???

Noah Memree
Principal

APPLETON ELEMENTARY SCHOOL

314 Apple Pie Avenue ⊚ Appleton, Illinois 61428

**"We aim to grow with excellence and avoid
branching out unless absolutely necessary"**

To: Noah Memree

From: Gladys Friday

Subject: RE: RE: New librarian

Date: August 14

Dear Mr. Memree,

Yes, new librarian. As you might recall, we received money to pay for a school librarian from a When All Else Fails Grant. You hired Ms. Danjerous on the last day of school. Remember?

What should I tell her about her daughter? And the library? The room that used to be our library is piled high with extra desks and chairs. All the books had to be thrown out because of mold. Remember?

Gladys Friday

Gladys Friday
Appleton Elementary School Secretary

APPLETON ELEMENTARY SCHOOL

314 Apple Pie Avenue ◎ Appleton, Illinois 61428

"We aim to grow with excellence and avoid branching out unless absolutely necessary"

To: Gladys Friday

From: Noah Memree

Subject: RE: RE: RE: New librarian

Date: August 17

Ms. Friday:

Oh, right. I forgot.

Tell Ms. Danjerous she can put her books in the first-floor broom closet. That should be big enough for a library.

You can also tell her we have plenty of room for another student. Last time I checked, we had only three children signed up for fifth grade. Let's hope the new school board president can help boost enrollment.

Carry on.

Noah Memree
Principal

APPLETON ELEMENTARY SCHOOL

314 Apple Pie Avenue ⊙ Appleton, Illinois 61428

"We aim to grow with excellence and avoid branching out unless absolutely necessary"

DAILY APPLE

you all the juicy news, even when it's rotten to the core

er & Editor   50 cents   Wednesday, August 19

App ton Has a New School Board President

by Etta Toryal

Appleton has a new school board president. Ivana Beprawpa was elected yesterday to a four-year term, beginning immediately. The small business owner has big ideas on how to improve public education in Appleton.

"I intend to bring back manners and morals," said Beprawpa at a victory party held at her clothing shop in downtown Appleton. "The simple words *please* and *thank you* are what separate us from the beasts of the jungle. Let's all try to be more polite this year, shall we? Thank you!"

Beprawpa takes over as school board president at a critical time in Appleton Elementary history. With enrollment at a record low, it's unclear how, or if, the school can keep its doors open. Under Illinois law, a public school must have at least 20 students enrolled at all times.

"If we don't have a school, we might as well not have a town," said Beprawpa. "But I'm confident that under my leadership, Appleton will not only survive but thrive."

Ivana Beprawpa hopes to bring back manners and morals.

Appleton's population has dropped significantly in recent years. So has interest in public education. As a result, Beprawpa is not only Appleton's school board president, she's the entire school board.

School Library Reopens After 14 Years

by Etta Toryal

For the first time in 14 years, Appleton Elementary will have a school library. The only problem is, there are no books and very little shelf space.

"No worries," says librarian Rita B. Danjerous, a recent transplant to Appleton. "I brought my own books. I'm excited to share them with students."

Ms. Danjerous has a daughter, May, who will be in fifth grade.

Continued on page 2, column 1

LIBRARY *Continued from page 1, column 1*

"We always welcome new students to our school," said Principal Noah Memree. "We're especially grateful for May's arrival. Without her, our total enrollment would be nineteen, and we'd be forced to close the school."

Rita B. Danjerous will be the new school librarian.

School Uniforms Now Required at Appleton Elementary
by Etta Toryal

Students model new school uniforms.

In addition to bringing back manners and morals, School Board President Ivana Beprawpa is also bringing back school uniforms.

"We lost our way when we started letting students decide what to wear to school," Beprawpa said.

Beginning tomorrow, the first day of school at Appleton Elementary, girls will be required to wear navy blue dresses and white gloves. Boys will wear tuxedo jackets and bow ties.

School uniforms are available at Beprawpa Attire in downtown Appleton.

Letter to the Editor

Dear Ms. Etta Toryal,

I've been reading *The Daily Apple* since I was five years old. I like knowing what's happening in town, even when the news is rotten to the core.

Now more than ever, it's important to pay attention to local news. For example, Appleton Elementary is facing hard times and an uncertain future. Can our school survive?

If you need a reporter who's not afraid to ask hard questions, let me know.

Sincerely,
Sarah Bellum

P.S. I'm 10 years old and just starting fifth grade. Hope that's not a problem.

THE DAILY APPLE

Bringing you all the juicy news, even when it's rotten to the core

316 Apple Pie Avenue
Appleton, Illinois 61428

Etta Toryal
Publisher & Editor

August 20

Sarah Bellum
c/o Appleton Elementary School
314 Apple Pie Avenue
Appleton, Illinois 61428

Dear Sarah,

I was delighted to receive your letter. As this newspaper's publisher, editor, and only reporter until now, I'm sure there are lots of good stories I'm missing. I have a hunch you're *just* the reporter I need to find and share important news with readers.

I can't wait to read your stories!

Sincerely,

Etta Toryal

Etta Toryal

P.S. You're just the right age for the job.

FIRST BANK OF APPLETON

Because Money Doesn't Grow on Trees

207 Apple Fritter Street   Penny Counter
Appleton, Illinois 61428   Loan Officer

August 21

Ivana Beprawpa
Owner, Beprawpa Attire
328 Baked Brie with Apples Avenue
Appleton, Illinois 61428

Dear Ms. Beprawpa,

Congratulations on your election to the school board. Consider this a friendly (and polite) reminder that your $5,000 loan is due today. Please stop by and pay the money you owe so that we can settle your account.

Have a great school year!

Sincerely,

Penny Counter

Penny Counter

Beprawpa Attire

Where Appleton Shops à la Mode
328 Baked Brie with Apples Avenue

Gloves, Gowns, Ties & Tuxedos
Appleton, Illinois 61428

Ivana Beprawpa
Proprietress

August 22

Penny Counter
First Bank of Appleton
207 Apple Fritter Street
Appleton, Illinois 61428

Dear Ms. Counter,

How lovely to hear from you, darling! A letter in the mail is always a joy to my heart.

Regarding the money your bank provided to me and which I used to produce tasteful campaign yard signs: I was under the impression that was a friendly donation to my campaign. Surely you're as concerned as I am about saving Appleton Elementary School. If the school goes under, your bank will be right behind it.

If you could simply reclassify my loan as a campaign contribution, we could consider this matter closed. It would be a great and polite kindness to me.

What do you say, dear?

Yours with impeccable manners,

Ivana Beprawpa

Ivana Beprawpa

P.S. In case you didn't know, the job of school board president is unpaid. I don't make a thin dime for my service to this community.

FIRST BANK OF APPLETON

Because Money Doesn't Grow on Trees

207 Apple Fritter Street
Appleton, Illinois 61428

Penny Counter
Loan Officer

August 24

Ivana Beprawpa
Owner, Beprawpa Attire
328 Baked Brie with Apples Avenue
Appleton, Illinois 61428

Dear Ms. Beprawpa,

I apologize if there was any confusion. The $5,000 you borrowed from this bank was *not* a gift, a donation, or a campaign contribution. It was a loan, pure and simple. As such, it must be paid back in full.

The loan was due last Friday, but as a "polite kindness," I can give you an extension until September 15.

In return, will you do a favor for me? I have a daughter in fourth grade who told me the new librarian has something called a "green dot collection" of books. I'm not sure I approve. Could you look into this?

Thank you for your generous and unpaid service to our community.

Penny Counter

Penny Counter

FOR **Noah Memree**

DATE **August 25** TIME **1:07** A.M. / P.M.

Urgent ☐

While You Were Out

M~~S~~. **Ivana Beprawpa**

OF _____

PHONE **746-4301**

AREA CODE — NUMBER — EXTENSION

TELEPHONED		PLEASE CALL	X
CAME TO SEE YOU		WILL CALL AGAIN	
RETURNED YOUR CALL		WANTS TO SEE YOU	

MESSAGE _____

Ivana Beprawpa
called. Wants to know
"What's up with the
green dot collection"
in the library.

SIGNED **G.F.**

9711

AUG 27 REID DURR > BEN THINKEN 9:24 AM
no questions asked
really?
yes
it's called the green dot collection
i don't get it
never mind
i'm going to get the book right now
we can read it after school

DURR'S ORCHARD

Delicious Apples   Homemade Cider   Select Fruits & Veggies

Highway PB at Apple Blossom Road
Appleton, Illinois 61428

Cyrus "Cy" Durr
Founder and Owner

August 28

Ivana Beprawpa
Beprawpa Attire
328 Baked Brie with Apples Avenue
Appleton, Illinois 61428

Dear Ms. Beprawpa,

Congratulations on your recent election. If you ever want to talk about school fund-raisers, let me know. I'd be happy to organize an apple-picking contest or a hay wagon ride. My son Reid (fifth grade) had his birthday party here last week and all the kids had a blast.

Speaking of Reid: I found him reading in bed last night with a flashlight at eleven o'clock. He wouldn't tell me the name of the book. Just said it was from the school's "green dot collection," whatever that means.

I don't know what a green dot collection is, but I'm not sure I like it, especially here in Appleton, home of the giant *red* apples. Just my opinion.

Sincerely,

Cy Durr

15

Where Appleton Shops à la Mode
328 Baked Brie with Apples Avenue

Gloves, Gowns, Ties & Tuxedos
Appleton, Illinois 61428

Ivana Beprawpa
Proprietress

August 31

Cy Durr
Durr's Orchard
Highway PB at Apple Blossom Road
Appleton, Illinois 61428

Dear Mr. Durr,

Thank you for your thoughtful letter. As school board president, I'm trying to bring back manners and morals. Let's leave the tacky fund-raisers to others, shall we?

I have heard of the green dot collection. I'm trying to get to the bottom of it. I agree it's a problem if books are interfering with children's sleep and/or our town's wholesome image.

Let me see what I can find out.

Yours with impeccable manners,

Ivana Beprawpa

Ivana Beprawpa

FOR Noah Memree

Urgent ☐

DATE September 1   **TIME** 10:25 (A.M.) P.M.

While You Were Out

M S. Ivana Beprawpa

OF

PHONE 746-4301

AREA CODE   NUMBER   EXTENSION   ☒

TELEPHONED		PLEASE CALL	
CAME TO SEE YOU		WILL CALL AGAIN	
RETURNED YOUR CALL		WANTS TO SEE YOU	

MESSAGE Ivana Beprawpa
called again.
(second time)
She's concerned about the green dot collection in library.
G.F.

9711

SIGNED

Beprawpa Attire

Where Appleton Shops à la Mode
328 Baked Brie with Apples Avenue

Gloves, Gowns, Ties & Tuxedos
Appleton, Illinois 61428

Ivana Beprawpa
Proprietress

September 3

Noah Memree
Appleton Elementary School
314 Apple Pie Avenue
Appleton, Illinois 61428

Dear Mr. Memree,

I've called several times and stopped by the school just now, but I can't seem to catch you. I wanted to tell you that I've heard from several parents about a "green dot collection" of books in the school library. Can you please find out what this is?

Thank you and have a polite day.

Ivana Beprawpa

Ivana Beprawpa

P.S. While at school, I noticed a girl wearing fingerless gloves. She looked like a scruffy orphan out of a Charles Dickens novel. Please remind all students that school uniforms are mandatory and available only at Beprawpa Attire. Thank you.

📄 Reply 📑 Reply All

To: Gladys Friday

From: Noah Memree

Subject: Green dot collection?

Date: September 8

Ms. Friday:

Find out what the green dot collection is all about.

Noah Memree
Principal

APPLETON ELEMENTARY SCHOOL
314 Apple Pie Avenue ◎ Appleton, Illinois 61428
"We aim to grow with excellence and avoid
branching out unless absolutely necessary"

To: Noah Memree

From: Gladys Friday

Subject: RE: Green dot collection?

Date: September 8

Dear Mr. Memree,

Have you forgotten we're supposed to be using our best manners this year? An occasional "please" or "thank you" would be appreciated. It would also set a good example for students.

Thank you.

Gladys Friday

Gladys Friday
Appleton Elementary School Secretary

APPLETON ELEMENTARY SCHOOL

314 Apple Pie Avenue ◉ Appleton, Illinois 61428

"We aim to grow with excellence and avoid branching out unless absolutely necessary"

To: Gladys Friday

From: Noah Memree

Subject: RE: RE: Green dot collection?

Date: September 9

Ms. Friday:

Please find out what the green dot collection is all about. Thank you. Also, Ivana Beprawpa says we have a female student wearing the wrong kind of white gloves. Find out who it is and give her a warning. Please and thank you.

Noah Memree
Principal

APPLETON ELEMENTARY SCHOOL

314 Apple Pie Avenue ◉ Appleton, Illinois 61428

"We aim to grow with excellence and avoid
branching out unless absolutely necessary"

MEMO FROM THE OFFICE

September 9

Dear Ms. Danjerous,

My apologies for not having time to properly welcome you to Appleton Elementary. I hope you're settling in and enjoying your work in the "library." It's a bit pathetic, isn't it? I admire your willingness to create a library from scratch.

Quick question: The principal had a letter from our new school board president. She asked about your "green dot collection" in the library. Can you please explain what it is? Thanks!

Also, I need you to fill out a form about your daughter. (See enclosed.) We have to get this information to the Illinois Department of Education if we want May officially enrolled at Appleton Elementary.

Sorry for the hassle. I hate paperwork as much as the next person, but it's my job to deal with this stuff.

Your friend in the office,

Gladys Friday

Gladys Friday
Appleton Elementary School Secretary

P.S. One more thing (sorry!): Just saw your daughter May in the hall. Her fingerless gloves are adorable, but the principal says they're not compliant with our new school uniform policy. Please pick up a pair of white gloves for her at Beprawpa Attire sometime soon, okay? Thanks!

APPLETON ELEMENTARY SCHOOL LIBRARY

September 10

Dear Ms. Friday,

"Ms. Danjerous" sounds so formidable. Please, call me Rita.

There's no need to apologize for not officially welcoming me to school. I know you're as busy as I am. Besides opening the library, I'm also settling into a new house and trying to make the transition as smooth as possible for my daughter.

Speaking of May, I'm enclosing the new student form with this letter. Please note that May's middle name is B without a period after it.

Thanks for the heads-up (or should I say *hands*-up?) on the glove situation. I hate to complain, but I'm a bit cash-strapped at the moment. New gloves are not high on my shopping list. (I'd rather buy books!) But don't worry. I'll find May another pair of gloves. I'm sure I have something suitable in one of my boxes of clothes.

You admire my willingness to create a library from scratch? I admire *your* ability to deal with all the paperwork involved in running a school. Would you like something more interesting to read at night? I'm leaving a few books in your mailbox. Let me know if you like them.

Your friend in the library,

Rita B. Danjerous

Rita B. Danjerous

P.S. Almost forgot: You asked about the green dot collection. Do you remember being young and having questions about things that felt embarrassing or scary or just plain weird—and not knowing where to turn for answers? I do. That's why I created my green dot collection. These are the books I wish I'd had when I was young and full of questions. If you have time after school, stop by the library. I'll brew us a pot of tea and tell you more!

NEW STUDENT FORM

Name of student: __May B Danjerous__
(First name) (Middle name) (Last name)

Age: __10__   Grade: __5th__

Home address: __1322 Apple Tart Place__

__Appleton, Illinois 61428__

Name of parent/guardian (in case of emergency):

__Rita B. Danjerous__

Recent photo of student:

Gladys,
I'm running out
of shelf space
in my broom
closet library.
Is there a cart
somewhere I
could borrow?
Rita

THE DAILY APPLE

Bringing you all the juicy news, even when it's rotten to the core

Etta Toryal, Publisher & Editor   50 cents   Saturday, September 12

Danjerous Bookmobile Now in Service at Appleton Elementary

by Sarah Bellum

Rita B. Danjerous distributes books from refashioned bookmobile.

What do you do when you run out of shelf space in the library?

If you're Rita B. Danjerous, you turn an old applecart into a new bookmobile.

"My friend, Gladys Friday, found this darling applecart in a school storage shed," said Danjerous. "All I had to do was tighten a few bolts, add a coat of paint, and fill the cart with terrific books."

In the short time she's been librarian at Appleton Elementary, Ms. Danjerous has quickly become a popular member of the school community. Students are enjoying Danjerous's daily research questions and choosing projects to work on in pairs. Several fifth graders also commented on Danjerous's green dot collection of books, from which students can borrow without having to use their school library cards.

"As children grow older, they become curious about many things, including subjects that might make them feel shy or embarrassed," explained Danjerous. "I like to keep a shelf reserved for books that tackle these topics. If students are interested, they can borrow any book with a green dot on the spine by simply slipping the book into their backpack and returning it when they're ready. Of course, if someone wants to check out a book from my green dot collection using their library card, that's fine, too."

So far, no one has. Students seem to prefer the more surreptitious approach of borrowing books without a library card.

Gladys Friday Late on Friday

by Sarah Bellum

School secretary stayed up too late reading.

Stop the presses!

Gladys Friday, Appleton Elementary School secretary, reported late to work yesterday for the first time in 17 years.

"I can't believe I overslept," said Friday. "Or maybe I can believe it. I was up until three o'clock in the morning, reading the most amazing mystery."

When asked to describe it, Friday said: "Oh my goodness, I can't even begin to describe that book. It was almost too good. I've never read anything like it in my whole life. I can't wait to ask Rita if she has any other books by the same author. If so, I'm going to read them all. But maybe I'll wait for the weekend, just in case."

When Danjerous heard about Friday's tardy arrival, she said: "Maybe I should feel bad that the book was so good, it kept her up all night." Then she smiled and added: "But I don't."

Danjerous noted she has plenty of books guaranteed to keep children awake past their bedtime, too.

"Some of the edgier books are in the green dot collection," she said. "Others are part of my regular collection. I encourage everyone to stop by the library and pick out a book that looks impossible to put down. I also have flashlights available for those who like to read under the covers."

Meet May B Danjerous

by Sarah Bellum

Welcome to the first in a series of interviews I plan to do with local residents. Today's interview is with the newest student at Appleton Elementary, May B Danjerous.

Sarah: Thanks for agreeing to do this interview!

May: You're welcome.

Sarah: How do you like our school?

May: So far so good. Everybody's been really nice to me.

Sarah: Glad to hear that. Do you think manners and morals can save our school?

May: I have no idea. Maybe you should interview the new school board president.

Sarah: That's a great idea. Want to help? We could be reporters together.

May: Sure, if it's okay with your boss.

Sarah: I'll find out. In the meantime, I have a question for you. I noticed you and your mom

May B Danjerous is interviewed by Sarah Bellum.

have the same middle initial. What's the B stand for?

May: In my mom's name, it stands for Bea (B-E-A). My middle name is just B without a period.

Sarah: That's cool. Hey, I keep meaning to tell you: I love your fishnet gloves.

May: Thanks! You can borrow them anytime.

FIRST BANK OF APPLETON

Because Money Doesn't Grow on Trees

207 Apple Fritter Street
Appleton, Illinois 61428

Penny Counter
Loan Officer

September 14

Ivana Beprawpa
Owner, Beprawpa Attire
328 Baked Brie with Apples Avenue
Appleton, Illinois 61428

Dear Ms. Beprawpa,

Just a quick, friendly, and polite reminder that tomorrow is
September 15, the day your $5,000 loan is due.

Please stop by at your convenience and repay the loan so
that we can settle this matter.

Politely yours,

Penny Counter

Penny Counter

P.S. Did you ever find out about the green dot collection?

Where Appleton Shops à la Mode   Gloves, Gowns, Ties & Tuxedos
328 Baked Brie with Apples Avenue   Appleton, Illinois 61428

Ivana Beprawpa
Proprietress

September 15

Penny Counter
First Bank of Appleton
207 Apple Fritter Street
Appleton, Illinois 61428

Dear Ms. Counter,

Thank you for your lovely letter. You might be interested to know that I have a calendar and am fully aware that my loan is due today.

Are *you* aware, Ms. Counter, how much time is required of a school board president? I spend every waking moment responding to concerns of parents like you. (Please note: I am *not* complaining. That would be uncouth.)

You asked about the green dot collection in the school library. Believe me when I tell you it is *far* more serious than you or anyone possibly knew.

According to a recent edition of *The Daily Apple*, students can borrow books from the green dot collection *without properly checking them out*. They just slip the books into their backpacks and away they go, like little hoodlums or shoplifters.

That's not all.

Did you hear about Gladys Friday arriving late to school on Friday because she'd stayed up half the night reading a book? Same thing happened with Cy Durr's son. Any book that keeps a person awake past nine o'clock is, to my mind, suspicious and almost certainly improper.

I assure you I will get to the bottom of this. In the meantime, please be patient about my loan. My business sales are not as strong this month as I'd like, even though we now have a school uniform policy in place. Need I mention whose daughter has not yet purchased proper gloves from me?

That's the librarian's daughter wearing fishnet gloves.

I think she's wearing fishnet stockings, too. Gah!

that ... flashlights available for those who like to read under the covers."

May B Danjerous is interviewed by Sarah Bellum.

have the same middle initial. What's the B stand for?
May: In my mom's name it stands for Bea (B-E ...

Call me old-fashioned, but I happen to think fishnet gloves are vulgar. No surprise this is the girl whose mother is pushing indecent books.

I shall be in touch again when I have more information about this troubling situation.

Yours in unpaid service to our children and community,

Ivana Beprawpa

Ivana Beprawpa

P.S. The same two fifth-grade girls just stopped by and asked to interview me. Call me hard-hearted, but I said, "No proper uniforms? No interview."

FIRST BANK OF APPLETON

Because Money Doesn't Grow on Trees

207 Apple Fritter Street
Appleton, Illinois 61428

Penny Counter
Loan Officer

September 16

Ivana Beprawpa
Owner, Beprawpa Attire
328 Baked Brie with Apples Avenue
Appleton, Illinois 61428

Dear Ms. Beprawpa,

Oh my goodness, I had *no* idea the green dot collection contained "those" kinds of books. Please, please, *please* do what you can to eradicate that *filth* from our school!

I'm extending your loan deadline to October 15. I'm also approving another $5,000 loan to keep your business afloat. Don't even try to thank me. It's the least I can do to support your tireless service to this community.

Gratefully yours,

Penny Counter

Penny Counter

P.S. You're *not* being hard-hearted with those fifth-grade girls. I applaud your old-fashioned values. Someone has to teach these children that life has *rules*!

FIRST BANK OF APPLETON

LOAN

Borrower's name: Ivana Beprawpa
Borrower's business: Beprawpa Attire
Amount of new loan: $5,000
Current balance owed on past loan(s): $5,000
Total due: $10,000
Due date: October 15

Approved by loan officer _Penny Counter_
Penny Counter

FIRST BANK OF APPLETON

2830

Pay to the
order of Ivana Beprawpa

Five thousand and 00/100 $ 5,000.00

Sept 16

Memo _____ Dollars

Bill Fold
President of First Bank of Appleton

To: Etta Toryal   CC: May B Danjerous

From: Sarah Bellum

Subject: Two questions

Date: September 17

Hi, Ms. Toryal!

Thanks again for letting me be a reporter. I'm having so much fun!

Is it OK if my new friend, May B Danjerous, works on stories with me? She suggested we try to get an interview with Ivana Beprawpa. We stopped by Ms. Beprawpa's shop on Tuesday, but she refused to talk to us until May buys a "proper" pair of white gloves for school.

We're not giving up, but I was wondering: Do you have any advice on interviewing someone who refuses to be interviewed?

Sarah Bellum
Fifth-Grade Reporter
Appleton Elementary School

To: Sarah Bellum; May B Danjerous

From: Etta Toryal

Subject: RE: Two questions

Date: September 18

Sarah and May:

I'm delighted you two want to work together. It'll be great to have two reporters working the Appleton Elementary School beat.

Getting people to talk is often the hardest part of journalism. Here's a thought: Did you know the school board holds monthly meetings? By law, these meetings must be open to the public. You two could attend a school board meeting and take notes on what Ivana Beprawpa says.

I look forward to reading your next article!

Etta Toryal
Publisher & Editor
The Daily Apple

Where Appleton Shops à la Mode
328 Baked Brie with Apples Avenue

Gloves, Gowns, Ties & Tuxedos
Appleton, Illinois 61428

Ivana Beprawpa
Proprietress

September 19

Noah Memree
Appleton Elementary School
314 Apple Pie Avenue
Appleton, Illinois 61428

Dear Mr. Memree,

The first school board meeting under my reign is scheduled for September 25. One topic that's certain to come up is the green dot collection in your school library.

As I see it, we have several options. We could work with law enforcement officials to impose a curfew on reading. Perhaps no reading after nine o'clock in the evening? That seems like a polite time for children (and school secretaries) to turn off the lights. Imposing a curfew could cause a kerfuffle, though, and it wouldn't solve the problem of children borrowing books without the proper use of a library card.

This is why I think the better approach is to demand that the new librarian simply do away with her green dot collection. It's too loosey-goosey, if you'll pardon the vernacular. You must impart on the librarian the importance of establishing strict rules and enforcing them. If I've said it once, I've said it a million times: *Things must be done in the proper fashion.*

That brings me to the matter of school uniforms: I notice there are still some students who are not in compliance with our new uniform policy. What is the point of having rules if we don't enforce them?

Mr. Memree, children *need* boundaries. Now, more than ever, with parents refusing to parent (don't even get me started), it's up to *us* as educators and concerned citizens to let children know what we expect of them. Proper use of a library card! Proper uniforms for school! This is just the beginning.

If we can emphasize these and other homegrown values, maybe we can save Appleton Elementary School. If we can't, we will have to live with the knowledge that we were unwilling to do the hard work of democracy.

Let's get this sorted out now so that I can report my progress to the community at my first school board meeting.

Yours with impeccable manners,

Ivana Beprawpa

Ivana Beprawpa

To: Gladys Friday

From: Noah Memree

Subject: This and that

Date: September 21

Ms. Friday:

There's a long letter on my desk from Ivana Beprawpa. I don't have time to read it. Will you? Please?

Also, someone from the Illinois Department of Education called. He needs the full and legal middle name (not the middle initial) of our new fifth grader. Can you take care of that? Please?

If you need me, I'll be writing demerits for school uniform violations.

Noah Memree
Principal

APPLETON ELEMENTARY SCHOOL

314 Apple Pie Avenue ◉ Appleton, Illinois 61428

"We aim to grow with excellence and avoid branching out unless absolutely necessary"

To: Noah Memree

From: Gladys Friday

Subject: RE: This and that

Date: September 21

Dear Mr. Memree,

Rita told me her daughter's middle name is B. It would be rude to ask again, but I'll let her know about Ms. Beprawpa's concern regarding the green dot collection. You're welcome.

If you need me, I'll be rolling my eyes at the thought of you giving the first demerit of the year to our newest student. (Sheesh.) Remember, you *could* just give her a gentle warning.

Gladys Friday
Gladys Friday
Appleton Elementary School Secretary

APPLETON ELEMENTARY SCHOOL
314 Apple Pie Avenue ⊚ Appleton, Illinois 61428
**"We aim to grow with excellence and avoid
branching out unless absolutely necessary"**

OFFICIAL DEMERIT
"DON'T BE A ROTTEN APPLE"

Appleton School District

May B Danjerous was seen _wearing the wrong style of gloves_ on _September 21_. This is a violation of _our elementary school uniform policy_ and will result in _a gentle warning_.

Noah Memree

Noah Memree

September 21

Ms. Danjerous (and Mom):

We looked up the official
uniform policy on the school
website. Here's what it says:
"Boys are required to wear a
black tuxedo jacket with a
bow tie in any tasteful color
or pattern. Girls are required
to wear a navy blue dress
and white gloves." So
Fishnet gloves are white. So
why are they "wrong"?

Sarah   May

Noah Momroe

MEMO FROM THE OFFICE

September 22

Dear Rita,

Hello, friend! How do you like my new memo stationery? You inspired me!

I'm writing to ask if you've had a chance to pick up new gloves for May yet. I know you're busy getting settled in at your new house and job, but I don't want May to get a demerit for a school uniform violation.

I'd be happy to stop by Beprawpa Attire after school today and buy the gloves. Just let me know May's glove size. Consider it my gift to you for introducing me to my new favorite author. (I found the books you left on my desk this morning. Thank you!)

Now here's the awkward part of this memo: Mr. Memree is getting some pushback from the school board president about your green dot collection in the library. She doesn't like the "loosey-goosey" approach to borrowing books. Apparently she's hearing from parents who say their kids are staying up too late reading. It's sure to come up at the school board meeting on Friday.

Anyway, just wanted you to know. Personally, I *like* the green dots. In all my years at Appleton, I've never seen students so excited about reading. Shouldn't we see that as a *good* thing?

Your friend in the front office,

Gladys ☺

Appleton Elementary School Secretary

APPLETON ELEMENTARY SCHOOL LIBRARY

September 23

Dear Gladys,

I love the new look of your memos! I also love how thoughtful you are to offer to pick up gloves for May.

But here's the thing: May and Sarah looked up the official uniform policy on the school website. There's nothing that says what kind of white gloves the girls must wear, so I'm not going to worry about it. May likes my fishnet gloves. Now that I think about it, I'm sure I have a pair of vintage white leather gloves somewhere she might like even better.

Back to books: I agree that getting students excited about reading is a *good* thing. My only problem is these kids are so hungry for books, I'm afraid I'm going to run out. Mr. Memree said there's no money in the budget for new books. Do you have any fundraising ideas?

Wondering in the library,

Rita B. Danjerous

P.S. Do you like being called a secretary? If so, great! If not, what about Executive Administrative Assistant Extraordinaire? To my mind, that sounds more like you!

MEMO FROM THE OFFICE

September 23

Rita,

Talk to Cy Durr about fund-raisers. He owns the orchard on the edge of town. He's always doing fun stuff with the kids.

Gladys ☺ ☺

Appleton Elementary School
Executive Administrative Assistant Extraordinaire

Gladys Friday

Executive Administrative Assistant
Extraordinaire

Appleton Elementary School

THE DAILY APPLE

Bringing you all the juicy news, even when it's rotten to the core

Etta Toryal, Publisher & Editor $1.50   Sunday, September 27

Book Lovers "Pick" a Juicy Fund-Raiser

by Etta Toryal

What's more fun than picking apples? How about picking new books from money raised by picking apples? If that sounds confusing, it wasn't, says orchard owner Cy Durr.

"Rita B. Danjerous stopped by the orchard on Friday," said Durr. "She asked if I had any chores she and the students could do to make money to buy library books. Her timing couldn't have been better. I'd just heard from a grocery store owner in Chicago who wanted a hundred bushels of apples. I told the librarian I'd pay ten dollars for every bushel she and the kids picked."

Danjerous and her fellow bookworms picked 100 bushels yesterday, raising $1,000 for the library.

"It was super fun," said Ben Thinken, a fifth-grade student who worked alongside his friend Reid Durr.

"Ben and I probably would've done it for free, just to spend some time together," said Reid.

Danjerous insisted on paying the pickers, but not with money. "I'm going to let the stu-

Danjerous and students pick apples for books at Durr's Orchard.

dents select our new books," said Danjerous. "I can't wait to see what titles they order. I also can't wait to come back to this orchard sometime. I'd love the grand tour."

"That could be arranged," said Cy Durr with a smile.

First School Board Meeting Ends on a Sour Note

by Etta Toryal

The Appleton School Board met Friday night in the Appleton Elementary cafeteria. School Board President Ivana Beprawpa opened the meeting with a speech.

"I've been delighted to hear more *please*s and *thank you*s from our local children," she began. "But I'm concerned about the manners of some adults at this school. It wouldn't be proper to speak ill of anyone in public, but I must ask every teacher and especially every librarian to please enforce our school rules, especially when it comes to providing proper reading material to children and following approved book-borrowing policies. We can't

let people come to our town and rewrite the rules willy-nilly."

Beprawpa said it's the lack of clear rules that's driven down Appleton's population and school enrollment. "It's lower than ever," she said sadly.

Principal Noah Memree said enrollment will increase by one as soon as a new student's paperwork is filled out correctly.

"New student?" said Beprawpa. "That must be the librarian's daughter. She's the girl wearing the vulgar fishnet gloves."

Continued on page 2, column 1

MEETING *Continued from page 1, column 2*

Appleton Elementary Executive Administrative Assistant Extraordinaire Gladys Friday raised her hand to speak. "That's not true," she said. "Sarah's wearing the fishnet gloves now. May's rocking a pair of elbow-length white leather gloves. See? They're sitting over there in the corner, taking notes. Hi, girls!"

Beprawpa made a sour face and mumbled something unintelligible. When she finished, fifth-grade student May B Danjerous raised her hand.

"The school uniform policy doesn't specify what kind of gloves we must wear," said Danjerous. "It just says the gloves must be white."

"Then we'll change the policy!" said Beprawpa, looking happy for the first time all evening.

Sarah Bellum, also in fifth grade, held up her fishnet-gloved hand and said: "I thought we

Ivana Beprawpa speaks at school board meeting.

didn't want people changing the rules willy-nilly."

"Don't get sassy with me, young lady," snapped Beprawpa, before abruptly adjourning the meeting.

Meet Penny Counter

by Sarah Bellum and May B Danjerous

Welcome to another interview with an Appleton resident. Today we're talking to Penny Counter, loan officer at First Bank of Appleton.

Sarah: Thanks so much for making time for this interview.

Penny: You're welcome. I'm eager to hear your questions.

May: In your professional opinion, how healthy is our local economy?

Penny: Not very. I'm sure you've noticed the vacant houses and empty storefronts. You probably have a lot of empty desks at school, too.

Sarah: We do. Is there a connection between a weak economy and a struggling school?

Penny: Absolutely. There's a hand-in-glove relationship between education and the economy. Towns with good schools tend to attract more people and businesses. As the economy grows, schools receive more money and continue to improve. By the same token, communities with inferior schools suffer. People move away. Businesses close. Schools get less

Penny Counter talks dollars and sense.

money for books, equipment, and teachers. It's not good.

May: Are you hopeful about the future of Appleton?

Penny: Depends. If people continue to borrow money and repay the money they owe, we'll be in good shape. If people don't pay back the money they owe—we call that defaulting—it's bad for the bank, bad for the economy, and bad for schools. It also sets a lousy example for children. So, if you're concerned about our town and you're not repaying money you owe, you really should get yourself to the bank ASAP.

FIRST BANK OF APPLETON

Because Money Doesn't Grow on Trees

207 Apple Fritter Street
Appleton, Illinois 61428

Penny Counter
Loan Officer

September 28

Ivana Beprawpa
Owner, Beprawpa Attire
328 Baked Brie with Apples Avenue
Appleton, Illinois 61428

Dear Ms. Beprawpa,

Did you see my interview in yesterday's *Daily Apple*? I thought you'd appreciate my hand-in-glove analogy.

The girls who interviewed me had excellent manners. I think you should reconsider giving them an interview. Oh, and I can tell you the reason the librarian hasn't purchased gloves from your shop yet. She's broke. She has only $97 in her checking account. (That's confidential, so forget I told you.)

But don't forget this: Your loans are due October 15. The combined total is $10,000.

Sincerely and politely,

Penny Counter

Penny Counter

Beprawpa Attire

Where Appleton Shops à la Mode
328 Baked Brie with Apples Avenue

Gloves, Gowns, Ties & Tuxedos
Appleton, Illinois 61428

Ivana Beprawpa
Proprietress

September 29

Penny Counter
First Bank of Appleton
207 Apple Fritter Street
Appleton, Illinois 61428

Dear Ms. Counter,

Yes, I saw your interview in the newspaper. You're as subtle as a heart attack.

Look, if I had the money, I'd pay you back today. But I don't have the money. Frankly, I find it appalling that our flashy new school librarian can make $1,000 in a few hours at Cy Durr's orchard. Don't I wish I could hold a fund-raiser so I could pay off my…

Wait a minute. I just had an idea.

Ivana Beprawpa

Ivana Beprawpa

Where Appleton Shops à la Mode
328 Baked Brie with Apples Avenue

Gloves, Gowns, Ties & Tuxedos
Appleton, Illinois 61428

Ivana Beprawpa
Proprietress

September 30

Cy Durr
Durr's Orchard
Highway PB at Apple Blossom Road
Appleton, Illinois 61428

Dear Mr. Durr,

I need to organize a fund-raiser. I don't have time to go into the details, but I need to make $10,000 fast. If I rounded up a dozen or so students from Appleton Elementary, could I bring them out on a school bus and have them pick apples for you? You would pay me directly, of course.

Let me know when I can bring some children out for a wholesome field trip.

Ivana Beprawpa

Ivana Beprawpa

DURR'S ORCHARD

Delicious Apples   Homemade Cider   Select Fruits & Veggies

Highway PB at Apple Blossom Road
Appleton, Illinois 61428

Cyrus "Cy" Durr
Founder and Owner

October 1

Ivana Beprawpa
Beprawpa Attire
328 Baked Brie with Apples Avenue
Appleton, Illinois 61428

Dear Ivana,

Sorry, no can do.

Rita and the kids picked the last of my apples. Wow, do I have a revised opinion of that woman. She gave me a book that is hands-down the *best* book I have ever read! It's a nail-biting thriller. Frankly, I'm thrilled to have met that librarian. I think she might be really *great* for Appleton.

Do you know if she's married or dating anyone? If not, I'd like to ask her and her daughter to come for dinner some night with Reid and me.

Sincerely,

Cy Durr

October 2

Cy Durr
Durr's Orchard
Highway PB at Apple Blossom Road
Appleton, Illinois 61428

Dear Mr. Durr,

Your reading diet holds zero interest for me; your romantic life even less. What I'm interested in is making $10,000 quickly. Have you *nothing* I could force children to do that would make money for me?

I want an answer—immediately. Thank you.

Yours with impeccable manners, even when dealing with a looming financial crisis,

Ivana Beprawpa

Ivana Beprawpa

DURR'S ORCHARD

Delicious Apples   Homemade Cider   Select Fruits & Veggies

Highway PB at Apple Blossom Road
Appleton, Illinois 61428

Cyrus "Cy" Durr
Founder and Owner

October 6

Ivana Beprawpa
Beprawpa Attire
328 Baked Brie with Apples Avenue
Appleton, Illinois 61428

Dear Ivana,

I apologize for not getting back to you right away. I've had my nose in that thriller Rita gave me. By the way, I found out she's single. I'm thinking I should ask if she has any cookbooks I could borrow. Then, I could invite her and May over for dinner some night.

Anyway, back to your fund-raiser. I wish I could help, but all I have left from this year's harvest is a bumper crop of cucumbers. My son Reid has made them into pickles to sell at the weekend farmers' market. There's not a lot of money in pickles, but I want my son to learn the value of hard work. We'll see if he can wake up at five o'clock on Saturday morning.

Sincerely,

Cy Durr

Cy Durr

Where Appleton Shops à la Mode
328 Baked Brie with Apples Avenue

Gloves, Gowns, Ties & Tuxedos
Appleton, Illinois 61428

Ivana Beprawpa
Proprietress

October 7

Reid Durr
Durr's Orchard
Highway PB at Apple Blossom Road
Appleton, Illinois 61428

Dear Reid,

Are you *really* going to let your father wake you up at five o'clock on Saturday morning to sell pickles? I have a better idea.

Let me buy your pickles. I'll sell them as a fund-raiser. You get to sleep in. I get to make some money. What do you say?

Ivana Beprawpa

Ivana Beprawpa

REID DURR

October 9

Ivana Beprawpa
Beprawpa Attire
328 Baked Brie with Apples Avenue
Appleton, Illinois 61428

Dear Ms. Beprawpa,

My dad says there isn't a lot of profit potential in pickles, but he also said it's up to me how and where I sell them. If you really want the pickles, I could sell them to you for 25 cents each. I have 10,000 pickles.

Let me know if you're interested. Again, I should warn you that pickles aren't particularly profitable.

Reid Durr

Reid Durr

Ivana Beprawpa
Proprietress

October 10

Reid Durr
Durr's Orchard
Highway PB at Apple Blossom Road
Appleton, Illinois 61428

Dear Reid,

Don't be a fool. There's profit potential in everything. You just have to be smart and savvy like me and know how to run a business.

Deliver 10,000 pickles to my shop ASAP. I'll sell them for $1.25 each and make $1.00 of pure profit per pickle. I promise to repay you as promptly as possible.

Pleasantly,

Ivana Beprawpa

Ivana Beprawpa

DURR'S ORCHARD

Highway PB at Apple Blossom Road
Appleton, Illinois 61428

>─⋅◇⋅○⋅◇⋅─<

ORDER & INVOICE

Date: October 12

Bill To:

Ivana Beprawpa
Beprawpa Attire
328 Baked Brie with Apples Ave.
Appleton, Illinois 61428

Ship To:

Same

Quantity	Description	Unit Price	Amount
10,000	Dill pickles	$.25	$2,500
		TOTAL	**$2,500**

Payment due: 30 days

Please send payment to: Reid Durr
Highway PB at Apple Blossom Road
Appleton, Illinois 61428

MEDIA RELEASE
For Immediate Release to All Appleton News Organizations

EVERY DAY IS PICKLE DAY AT APPLETON ELEMENTARY!

Contact: Ivana Beprawpa
Release date: October 12

(Appleton, IL) Looking for a healthy after-school snack? Buy a premium dill pickle. These pickles won't last long. Get them while they last. Pickles cost only $1.25 each and are available every day after school on the Appleton Elementary playground. Why eat a sweet and gooey after-school snack when you can have a crisp and crunchy pickle? Yes, children, this is a snack that tastes great and is actually good for you! Ask your parents for extra money so you can buy pickles for all your friends. Don't miss this fabulous opportunity! If you have questions, see Ivana Beprawpa. She will be happy to sell you a pickle. Buy one for yourself. Buy twelve more to give to your family and friends. The future is pickles! Buy yours today!

FOR Noah Memree   **Urgent** ☐

DATE October 15   **TIME** 9:30 Ⓐ.Ⓜ. / P.M.

While You Were Out

Mr. Dewey A. Proove

OF _____

PHONE   843-7027

AREA CODE   NUMBER   EXTENSION

TELEPHONED		PLEASE CALL	☒
CAME TO SEE YOU		WILL CALL AGAIN	
RETURNED YOUR CALL		WANTS TO SEE YOU	

MESSAGE Dewey A. Proove
called from the
Illinois Department
of Education. Says
new student paper-
work is still
incomplete.

SIGNED G.F.

9711

...ree   **Urgent** ☐

TIME 11:45 Ⓐ.Ⓜ. / P.M.

...ere Out

... Proove

7027

EXTENSION

...CALL   ☒

RETURNED YOUR CALL		WILL CALL AGAIN	
		WANTS TO SEE YOU	

MESSAGE Dewey A. Proove
called again. Says
he needs final paper-
work on May B.
Danjerous if we
want her to be counted
in our total enrollment.

SIGNED G.F.

9711

FOR **Noah Memree**   **Urgent** ☒

DATE **October 19**   TIME **2:30**   A.M. / **P.M.**

While You Were Out

Mr. **Dewey A. Proove**

OF _____

PHONE **843-7027**

AREA CODE   NUMBER   EXTENSION

TELEPHONED		PLEASE CALL	☒
CAME TO SEE YOU		WILL CALL AGAIN	
RETURNED YOUR CALL		WANTS TO SEE YOU	

MESSAGE **Dewey A. Proove called again. Says if he doesn't get an answer, he'll have to come investigate.**

SIGNED **G.F.**

9711

To: Gladys Friday

From: Noah Memree

Subject: Can you do this?

Date: October 20

Ms. Friday:

Can you get back to the Illinois Department of Education? Please? Send whatever information they need. Thank you.

Noah Memree
Principal

APPLETON ELEMENTARY SCHOOL

314 Apple Pie Avenue ⊚ Appleton, Illinois 61428

"We aim to grow with excellence and avoid
branching out unless absolutely necessary"

To: Noah Memree

From: Gladys Friday

Subject: RE: Can you do this?

Date: October 20

Dear Mr. Memree,

I called Dewey A. Proove at the Illinois Department of Education. He says he cannot increase our enrollment by one student unless he has the full and legal middle name of May B Danjerous.

I've asked Rita B. Danjerous about this. She says B *is* May's full and legal middle name. I told Mr. Proove the same.

If you think you can get a better answer, I suggest you ask Rita or May, and then call Dewey A. Proove yourself.

Sincerely frustrated with you,

Gladys Friday

Gladys Friday
Appleton Elementary School
Executive Administrative Assistant Extraordinaire

APPLETON ELEMENTARY SCHOOL

314 Apple Pie Avenue ◉ Appleton, Illinois 61428

"We aim to grow with excellence and avoid
branching out unless absolutely necessary"

APPLETON ELEMENTARY SCHOOL

314 Apple Pie Avenue ....Appleton, Illinois 61428

"We aim to grow with excellence and avoid branching out unless absolutely necessary"

Mr. Noah Memree
Principal

October 22

Dear Ms. Danjerous,

I'll get right to the point.

This school has struggled in recent years with a rapid decline in enrollment. That was one of the reasons we were so happy to welcome your daughter, May, to Appleton Elementary School as a fifth grader.

Unfortunately, the Illinois Department of Education refuses to recognize her as a new student because officials claim we (meaning you) have not properly filled out the new student paperwork. Specifically, we (meaning they) need to know what the middle initial B. stands for in May's name. If the Department of Education refuses to recognize May as a new student, our enrollment will be listed as 19 students, and we will have to close our doors.

If you can provide me with May's middle name, I will continue to give her warnings rather than demerits for her school uniform violations. But you really need to buy your daughter a proper pair of white gloves. I'm worried what Ivana Beprawpa will say (or do) if she sees May wearing the wrong kind of gloves again.

Sincerely,

Noah Memree

Noah Memree

APPLETON ELEMENTARY SCHOOL LIBRARY

October 23

Dear Mr. Memree,

May's full and legal middle name is B, plain and simple, without a comma, without a period, without standing for a longer name. I told Gladys Friday this more than a month ago. Knowing Gladys, I'm sure she relayed the information to you.

Regarding Ivana Beprawpa: You can worry about her if you want. I haven't the time or the inclination. I'm too busy introducing students to some of my best friends in the world. Is it strange that many of these friends are found in books? I suppose I'm drawn to characters who worry less about making rules and more about making a difference in the world.

Speaking of books, have I got a good one for you! It's considered a cult classic among elementary school principals. I'll leave it in your mailbox. It's banned in many school districts for reasons you'll understand once you read it.

Your friend in the library,

Rita B. Danjerous

Rita B. Danjerous

THE DAILY APPLE

Bringing you all the juicy news, even when it's rotten to the core

Etta Toryal, Publisher & Editor   50 cents   Monday, October 26

Has Memree Remembered How to Read?

by Sarah Bellum and May B Danjerous

If you want to talk to Appleton Elementary School Principal Noah Memree, you might have to wait.

"Mr. Memree has been in his office with the door closed and locked since Friday afternoon," said Executive Administrative Assistant Extraordinaire Gladys Friday. "I think he spent the whole weekend there. He told me to hold his calls and cancel all his appointments."

Asked to speculate about what he might be doing behind his closed door, Friday shrugged. "Who knows?" she said. "All I can hear is the sound of him laughing like a hyena."

Meanwhile, says Friday, an official with the Illinois Department of Education has expressed concern about Appleton Elementary's enrollment. "Dewey A. Proove keeps calling," said Friday. "He's in charge of making sure all Illinois public schools are in compliance with the state's rules and regulations."

According to Friday, Proove is not satis-

Noah Memree's office door has been closed since Friday.

fied with the school's new student records. "I wouldn't be surprised if Mr. Proove pays a visit to Appleton when we least expect it."

Pickle Sales "Improperly Low," Says Beprawpa

by Etta Toryal

You could say she's disappointed. You could describe her as frustrated. But it might be more accurate to call Ivana Beprawpa just plain mad.

"Why aren't children buying my pickles?" Beprawpa wondered aloud Friday on the Appleton Elementary School playground.

Beprawpa has 10,000 pickles she's ready and eager to sell to Appleton Elementary students every day after school. But when the last bell rings, children seem to have other things they'd rather do.

"I like to stop by the library and see if Ms. Danjerous has added any new books to the green dot collection," said Ben Thinken, a fifth-grade student.

Continued on page 2, column 1

Ivana Beprawpa pushes pickles on students.

PICKLE *Continued from page 1, column 1*

"But pickles have little green dots!" said Beprawpa. "And pickles are healthier than those suspicious books you're reading! Buy a pickle, you little brat!"

Beprawpa then began chasing Thinken and his friend, Reid Durr, around the playground, waving a pickle at the boys. "Buy a pickle right now!" she yelled. "I politely yet firmly insist you buy a pickle!"

Meet Durr and Thinken

by Sarah Bellum and May B Danjerous

Welcome back to interviews with interesting people in Appleton. Today we're talking with fifth graders Reid Durr and Ben Thinken.

May: Hi, guys.

Reid and Ben: Hey, May! Hey, Sarah!

Sarah: You two have become so close this year, you even say *hey* the same way.

Reid: (Laughs) Not always.

Ben: We do have minds and voices of our own.

May: But you're best friends, right?

Reid: Absolutely.

Ben: We were best friends last year, too, but this year we're even better friends.

Sarah: How did that happen?

Ben: We have a lot in common.

Reid: That's true. Ben makes me laugh!

Ben: And we both love art and design.

Reid: Ben and I have been designing our own bow ties.

Reid Durr and Ben Thinken are best friends forever.

Ben: Ms. Danjerous said fashion design could be our research project this semester.

Sarah: Cool!

Ben: We'll show you our tie designs sometime, if you're interested.

May: Yes, please! We'd love to see them.

Sarah: Let's meet in the library after school.

BOW TIES FOR EVERY OCCASION

Green dot tie

Rainy day tie

I spy tie

Shoo-fly tie

Tie-dyed tie

Tic-tac-toe tie

Bow-wow tie

Pad tie

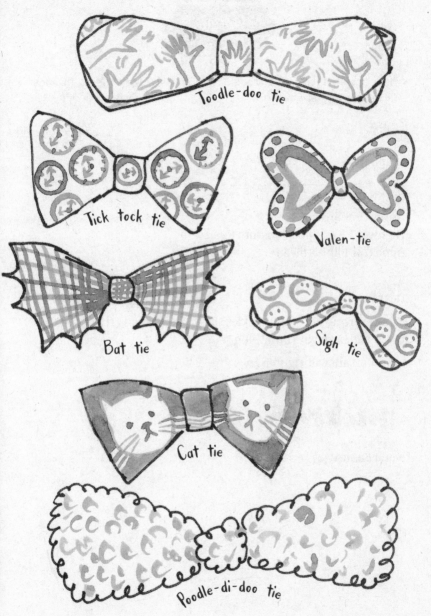

Toodle-doo tie

Tick tock tie

Valen-tie

Bat tie

Sigh tie

Cat tie

Poodle-di-doo tie

Sketches by Ben and Reid

Beprawpa Attire

Where Appleton Shops à la Mode
328 Baked Brie with Apples Avenue

Gloves, Gowns, Ties & Tuxedos
Appleton, Illinois 61428

Ivana Beprawpa
Proprietress

October 26

Reid Durr
Durr's Orchard
Highway PB at Apple Blossom Road
Appleton, Illinois 61428

Dear Reid,

What's wrong with your pickles? Kids aren't buying them. Was
this a bad batch or something?

I want an answer right away.

Ivana Beprawpa

Ivana Beprawpa

REID DURR

October 27

Ivana Beprawpa
Beprawpa Attire
328 Baked Brie with Apples Avenue
Appleton, Illinois 61428

Dear Ms. Beprawpa,

Sorry the pickles aren't selling. Maybe you need a better sign for your pickle stand. My friend Ben and I could make one for you. We're pretty good at designing stuff.

I'll ask around and see if anyone else has other ideas.

Good luck!

Reid Durr

Reid Durr

Sarah and May
Fifth-Grade Friends and Reporters
Appleton Elementary School
314 Apple Pie Avenue   Appleton, Illinois 61428

October 27

Ivana Beprawpa
Beprawpa Attire
328 Baked Brie with Apples Avenue
Appleton, Illinois 61428

Dear Ms. Beprawpa,

Reid says you're looking for ways to increase your pickle sales. Here's an idea: You could try to get pickles on the school lunch menu. If you get them on the menu every day for a week, that's twenty kids eating a pickle a piece per day. Multiplied by five days, that's a hundred pickles a week!

Maybe it's a silly idea, but it's worth a try.

Sincerely,

Sarah Bellum

May B Dangerous

Where Appleton Shops à la Mode
328 Baked Brie with Apples Avenue

Gloves, Gowns, Ties & Tuxedos
Appleton, Illinois 61428

Ivana Beprawpa
Proprietress

October 28

Noah Memree
Appleton Elementary School
314 Apple Pie Avenue
Appleton, Illinois 61428

Dear Mr. Memree,

I just had the most brilliant and original idea: Let's put pickles on the school lunch menu!

School lunches can be so dreary and disappointing. Mushy mashed potatoes. Limp green beans. Tuna salad with all the pizzazz of an old dishrag. Let's pep things up with pickles!

A smart man like you must know that pickles are an excellent source of nutrition. Plus, they're crunchy and crisp. And the word *pickles* is just fun to say. *Pickles, pickles, pickles!*

That's not all. The pickles I'm selling are made from Cy Durr's homegrown cucumbers, so we know they're delicious. After researching the little-known benefits of pickles, I think we should consider adding pickles to our breakfast menu, too. Scrambled eggs with pickles, anyone? Breakfast pickle tacos? Pickle pancakes? My mouth is watering already!

I'll enclose a complimentary pickle with this letter. Feast your taste buds on the homegrown taste of Appleton, and then give me a call at your earliest convenience.

Yours with impeccable manners—and now with impeccable pickles, too!

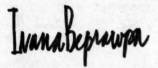

Ivana Beprawpa

P.S. On a more somber note: I saw in Monday's *Daily Apple* that you might be getting a visit from an official with the Illinois Department of Education. When he arrives, kindly inform him that we want a full investigation of Rita B. Danjerous. I'm telling you, that woman is a problem. So are her books—and her daughter. The child still hasn't been to my store to buy proper gloves!

MEMO FROM THE OFFICE

October 29

Ivana Beprawpa
Beprawpa Attire
328 Baked Brie with Apples Avenue
Appleton, Illinois 61428

Dear Ms. Beprawpa,

Mr. Memree is still in his office, reading and giggling, so I'll answer for him.

The Illinois Department of Education mandates what foods we can serve to students. If you want to get pickles on the menu, I suggest you contact Dewey A. Proove.

Thanks for the pickle.

Gladys Friday

Gladys Friday
Appleton Elementary School
Executive Administrative Assistant Extraordinaire

October 29

Ivana Beprawpa
Beprawpa Attire
328 Baked Brie with Apples Avenue
Appleton, Illinois 61428

Dear Ms. Beprawpa,

We had another idea for how you might boost your pickle sales. Let us interview you for *The Daily Apple*. You could tell us how you got interested in pickles. Maybe you'd even attract some adult customers who are looking for a healthy afternoon snack.

We hope you'll say yes to an interview!

Sincerely,

Sarah Bellum

May B Danjerous

Where Appleton Shops à la Mode   Gloves, Gowns, Ties & Tuxedos
328 Baked Brie with Apples Avenue   Appleton, Illinois 61428

Ivana Beprawpa
Proprietress

October 30

Sarah Bellum and May B Danjerous
Appleton Elementary School
314 Apple Pie Avenue
Appleton, Illinois 61428

Dear Girls,

Yes, I'd be happy to let you interview me for *The Daily Apple*—just as soon as every fifth-grade girl is in compliance with the school uniform dress code.

I might have to start writing demerits. Don't think I won't.

Sincerely serious,

Ivana Beprawpa

Ivana Beprawpa

Sarah and May
Fifth-Grade Friends and Reporters
Appleton Elementary School
314 Apple Pie Avenue   Appleton, Illinois 61428

November 2

Ivana Beprawpa
Beprawpa Attire
328 Baked Brie with Apples Avenue
Appleton, Illinois 61428

Dear Ms. Beprawpa,

Demerits don't count unless they're written on official stationery. So we've printed a box of stationery for you. You wouldn't want anyone to think you have a conflict of interest between your clothing business and your school board responsibilities.

Similarly sincerely serious,

May B Danjerous   *Sarah Bellum*

IVANA BEPRAWPA
SCHOOL BOARD PRESIDENT
APPLETON SCHOOL DISTRICT

This is an official demerit for _May B Danjerous_

for not wearing the proper style of gloves.

Ivana Beprawpa
Ivana Beprawpa

November 3
Date

IVANA BEPRAWPA
SCHOOL BOARD PRESIDENT
APPLETON SCHOOL DISTRICT

Here's another demerit for _May B Danjerous_

for not wearing proper gloves.

Ivana Beprawpa
Ivana Beprawpa

November 4
Date

IVANA BEPRAWPA
SCHOOL BOARD PRESIDENT
APPLETON SCHOOL DISTRICT

Here's a demerit for ___*Sarah Bellum*___ for buying proper gloves but not wearing them to school.

___*Ivana Beprawpa*___
Ivana Beprawpa

___*November 6*___
Date

IVANA BEPRAWPA
SCHOOL BOARD PRESIDENT
APPLETON SCHOOL DISTRICT

Here's another demerit for ___*May*___ . Tired of getting demerits? Then get your insubordinate self to my shop and buy a pair of proper white gloves.

___*Ivana Beprawpa*___
Ivana Beprawpa

___*November 9*___
Date

MEMO FROM THE OFFICE

November 9

Dear Rita,

I'm worried about May. She and Sarah were so sweet to print a whole box of stationery for Ivana Beprawpa, but now Ivana is using that stationery as a weapon. Have you seen the demerits she's given May and Sarah? I'm afraid Ivana's going to write to the Illinois Department of Education and make a formal complaint against *you*.

I realize the school uniform policy doesn't specify what kind of white gloves the girls should wear. I happen to love seeing May rock your elbow-length leather gloves. But wouldn't it be easier to buy her a pair of white cotton gloves from Ivana Beprawpa and be done with it?

I know what you're thinking. It's an unnecessary expense and you're already up to your eyeballs in expenses after your recent move. I totally understand! This is where friends come in handy.

Enclosed please find a gift certificate to Beprawpa Attire. It should be enough for one pair of gloves. I'd be happy to take May shopping some day after school this week. Let me know a good day.

Your friend in the front office,

Gladys

Appleton Elementary School
Executive Administrative Assistant Extraordinaire

GIFT CERTIFICATE

Where Appleton Shops à la Mode

Beprawpa
Attire

In the amount of _twenty-five dollars_ to be spent at Beprawpa Attire.

Ivana Beprawpa

Ivana Beprawpa
Proprietress

APPLETON ELEMENTARY SCHOOL LIBRARY

November 10

Dear Gladys,

How did I get so lucky to find a friend like you? Your thoughtfulness makes me misty-eyed. And if it were just about the money, I might accept your generous gift certificate—though, of course, I'd pay you back when I could.

But Gladys, this isn't about the money. It's the principle. I'm trying to raise my daughter to be a good, kind, curious person. That means following the rules, when appropriate. But it also means questioning rules and the people who make them.

In this case, the uniform policy doesn't stipulate what kind of white gloves the girls must wear. So why must we buy a pair of gloves from Beprawpa Attire? To my mind, that's blackmail.

If I sound upset about this, I'm really not. Maybe I should care about white gloves, but I'm too busy caring about this little library. The children are starting to *ask* for books. Adults are, too. When I came to school this morning, I found my desk covered with book requests. Do you know how happy that makes me?

I'm also happy to have a friend like you.

Yours with gratitude,

Rita B. Danjerous

I READ BANNED BOOKS
MS. DANJEROUS,
DO YOU HAVE ANY BOOKS ON THE HISTORY OF FASHION?
BEN
Dear Ms. Danjerous,
I'm looking for a book about. . . It's embarrass-ing, so I'm going to write it really small on the other side of this paper.
Anonymous
Hi, RBD! Can you please order some books on investigative journalism? I'm trying to learn how to follow the money.
Thanks! Sarah

IVANA BEPRAWPA

SCHOOL BOARD PRESIDENT
APPLETON SCHOOL DISTRICT
328 Baked Brie with Apples Avenue
Appleton, Illinois 61428

November 13

Dewey A. Proove
Illinois Department of Education
100 N. 1st Street
Springfield, Illinois 62777

Dear Mr. Proove,

I know you're a very important man and probably exceptionally intelligent and strong, too, so I'm confident you're the person who can help me with a serious problem that has been weighing heavily on my mind and heart.

It has come to my attention as school board president that the food our children are eating at Appleton Elementary is dull and unappealing. How many soggy grilled cheese sandwiches can we force down kids' throats?

Don't worry. I'm not one of those tiresome people who complain about a problem without offering a solution. I have the answer: Pickles!

I happen to have a few (well, more like *a lot* of) pickles I would be willing to part with in the interest of providing Appleton Elementary students with a crunchy, nutritious side dish for breakfast or lunch. For a limited time only, I am offering to sell you my pickles for $1.50 each. Or, I could sell you 10,000 pickles for the low, low price of $14,999. You can pay when you visit our school.

Yours with impeccable manners, impeccable pickles, and now an impeccable deal you won't be able to resist,

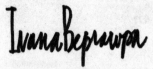

Ivana Beprawpa

P.S. When you visit Appleton Elementary, I'd like to talk to you about our new librarian. I'm sorry to say she is **not** a good fit for our school. If you can give me any ideas how to convince her to pack up her books and move on, I would be most grateful.

DEWEY A. PROOVE

Chief Compliance Officer **Illinois Dept. of Education**

100 N. 1st Street
Springfield, Illinois 62777

November 16

Ivana Beprawpa
School Board President
Appleton School District
328 Baked Brie with Apples Avenue
Appleton, Illinois 61428

Dear Ms. Beprawpa,

In reference to your letter:

- NO to pickles on the school lunch, breakfast, or snack menu.
- YES to speaking with you about your school librarian.
- BE AWARE that the purpose of my visit is to determine your school's total enrollment.

Officially,

Dewey A. Proove

Dewey A. Proove

To: Sarah Bellum; May B Danjerous

From: Etta Toryal

Subject: Muffins and cocoa?

Date: November 19

Sarah and May:

Just wanted to say hats off to you both for the excellent reporting you've done so far. I'm really impressed by the quality of your writing. As a thank you, may I treat you to cocoa and muffins at the Apple Cart Café next week?

Ivana Beprawpa wants to meet me at the café at 3:30 p.m. on Tuesday for an interview. I know how hard you two have been trying to get her to talk. Maybe I could introduce you to her after the interview. Are you available on Tuesday at 4:30ish for a quick hello with Ivana, followed by muffins and cocoa?

Etta Toryal
Publisher & Editor
The Daily Apple

Back

Reply ⬚ Reply All   Forward ⇨

To: Etta Toryal; May B Danjerous

From: Sarah Bellum

Subject: RE: Muffins and cocoa?

Date: November 20

Ms. Toryal:

Thanks for your nice message and the cocoa-and-muffins invitation. We accept!

May and I are out of school by 3:30. Could we meet you at the café then and sit in on your interview with Ivana Beprawpa? We'd love to watch a professional like you at work.

Sarah Bellum
Fifth-Grade Reporter
Appleton Elementary School

To: Etta Toryal; Sarah Bellum

From: May B Danjerous

Subject: RE: RE: Muffins and cocoa?

Date: November 20

Ms. Toryal:

Ivana won't grant us an interview on our own because we're not wearing "proper" white gloves. Maybe we could ask her a few questions while you're interviewing her. What do you think?

May B Danjerous
Fifth-Grade Reporter
Appleton Elementary School

To: May B Danjerous; Sarah Bellum

From: Etta Toryal

Subject: RE: RE: RE: Muffins and cocoa?

Date: November 21

Sarah and May:

I think it's an excellent idea! I'll meet you at the Apple Cart Café on Tuesday at 3:30 p.m. No gloves required.

Try not to laugh when Ivana pitches a Thanksgiving story. That's why she wants to meet with me. She claims the Pilgrims served pickles at the first Thanksgiving. We can discuss over muffins how quoting people directly can let readers make up their own minds about the news.

Etta Toryal
Publisher & Editor
The Daily Apple

THE DAILY APPLE

Bringing you all the juicy news, even when it's rotten to the core

Etta Toryal, Publisher & Editor   50 cents   Wednesday, November 25

This Thanksgiving, Replace Pumpkin with Pickles, Says Beprawpa

by Etta Toryal

Want to celebrate Thanksgiving like the Pilgrims? Serve pickles, says Ivana Beprawpa.

"It's a little-known fact, but the Pilgrims loved pickles," Beprawpa said in an interview yesterday at the Apple Cart Café. "Pilgrims brought pickles over on the *Mayflower* and served them at the first Thanksgiving. You know the song that begins, 'Oh, say can you see'? The next word is pickles. 'Oh, say can you see pickles'! Sadly, that part's been lost to history."

According to Beprawpa, pickles are perfect for Thanksgiving. "Pumpkins are so bland and mushy. Pickles are preferable. They're the perfect symbol of American democracy. Their crispness makes them stand tall and proud, like our great nation."

Beprawpa is selling pickles every afternoon on the Appleton Elementary playground. The cost is $1.25 per pickle. "If you love this town and this country, you really must buy at least one pickle," said Beprawpa.

According to Appleton Elementary librarian Rita B. Danjerous, purchasing pickles is not mandatory. In fact, not purchasing pickles might be more closely aligned with the spirit

Beprawpa says pickles are the perfect symbol of American democracy.

of American democracy. "This country was founded on the principles of dissent and resistance," said Danjerous. "No one can force anyone to buy a pickle."

As to whether or not the Pilgrims served pickles at the first Thanksgiving, Danjerous said she'd have to look into it. "Better yet, I'll have the fifth-grade class research it."

Sew What's New at the Library?

by Sarah Bellum

If you've got a problem, Rita B. Danjerous has a book for you. The Appleton Elementary librarian also has magazines, newspapers, and audiobooks available for borrowing.

As of yesterday, she has a sewing machine, too.

"I was taking a walk when I happened to glance in a second-hand shop," said Danjerous.

Continued on page 2, column 1

Danjerous oversees sewing project with two fifth-grade boys.

LIBRARY *Continued from page 1, column 1*

"This gorgeous old sewing machine was sitting in the window. It worked perfectly, so I bought it for the library. Why shouldn't students be able to borrow a sewing machine? I know some children who might really enjoy sewing their own clothes."

Two fifth-grade boys have already designed a dozen bow ties and are eager to borrow the library's sewing machine so they can create and wear them.

"Turns out the school uniform policy doesn't say what kind of bow ties we have to wear," said Reid Durr. "They just have to be 'tasteful.'"

"Taste is a matter of opinion," added Ben Thinken. "So we're going to return our old ties for a refund and use the money to buy fabric to make ties. If anyone wants to buy a bow tie from us, just return your old tie to Beprawpa Attire. Now that we have a sewing machine, we can make three ties for the price of one of Ivana Beprawpa's ties."

Meet Ivana Beprawpa

by Sarah Bellum and May B Danjerous

Ivana Beprawpa has a passion for pickles.

Today's interview is with Appleton School Board President Ivana Beprawpa.

Sarah: Thank you for agreeing to do this interview.

Ivana: Not like I had much of a choice. Why aren't you girls wearing proper school uniform gloves?

Sarah: Because we're not at school. We're at the café.

May: And because even when we are at school, the uniform policy doesn't specify what kind of gloves we have to wear.

Ivana: Blah blah blah. In my day, children did what adults told them to do.

May: Did that include buying pickles?

Ivana: Of course!

Sarah: How did you become so passionate about pickles?

Ivana: Well, I needed a good fund-raiser, er, I mean, fun raiser. Pickles are fun! They're also crunchy. I can't understand why you children won't buy my pickles after school.

May: A lot of kids go straight from their last class to the library to see if my mom has any new books in the green dot collection.

Ivana: Your mom and her stupid green dot collection. I should call for a boycott of the Appleton Elementary library.

Sarah: You want to boycott books?

Ivana: Yes! I want you children to enjoy life a little. After school you deserve a pickle!

May: They're a bit tricky to eat with proper manners. They can be loud and messy and—

Ivana: Oh, for crying out loud! Just buy my pickles! We'll worry about manners later.

IVANA BEPRAWPA

SCHOOL BOARD PRESIDENT
APPLETON SCHOOL DISTRICT
328 Baked Brie with Apples Avenue
Appleton, Illinois 61428

November 27

Noah Memree
Appleton Elementary School
314 Apple Pie Avenue
Appleton, Illinois 61428

<u>PERSONAL AND CONFIDENTIAL</u>

Dear Mr. Memree,

Gladys, I know you're reading this, so I'm going to say this once and only once: STOP READING. This is none of your business. Walk this letter into Mr. Memree's office RIGHT NOW. I don't care if the door's locked. You have a key to every room in that school. Use the key and open the door. Then put this letter on his desk and walk out.

You're still reading, Gladys! I know you are. Put the letter on his desk and walk out. Now!

Is she gone? Is it just you and me, Mr. Memree? Good. Now listen up.

You have to fire that Danjerous woman. Gladys will try to talk you out of it because they're friends, but don't listen to her. Listen to me. YOU MUST FIRE RITA B. DANJEROUS.

If you won't do it, I will. Send me her personnel file. I'll find some dirt on her. Trust me, I'm good at this. What did her previous employers say about her? Surely Appleton Elementary isn't her first rodeo. If she's been fired before, I want to know when, where, why, and especially HOW so I can fire her again. In fact, I want to talk to every principal of every school where she's ever worked. Send me her references. I will not take NO for an answer.

Yours with impeccable manners, impeccable pickles, and now an impeccable passion for propriety, particularly pedagogical public policy,

Ivana Beprawpa

Mr. Memree,
you might want
to read this.
GF

To: Gladys Friday

From: Noah Memree

Subject: Important

Date: November 30

Ms. Friday:

I need to see Ms. Danjerous's personnel file. I'm especially interested
in what her previous employers said
about her.

Noah Memree
Principal

APPLETON ELEMENTARY SCHOOL

314 Apple Pie Avenue ⦿ Appleton, Illinois 61428

**"We aim to grow with excellence and avoid
branching out unless absolutely necessary"**

To: Noah Memree

From: Gladys Friday

Subject: RE: Important

Date: November 30

Dear Mr. Memree,

You forgot the magic words.

Gladys Friday
Gladys Friday
Appleton Elementary School
Executive Administrative Assistant Extraordinaire

APPLETON ELEMENTARY SCHOOL
314 Apple Pie Avenue ◉ Appleton, Illinois 61428
"We aim to grow with excellence and avoid
branching out unless absolutely necessary"

To: Gladys Friday

From: Noah Memree

Subject: RE: RE: Important

Date: November 30

Ms. Friday:

I don't have time for games. I need to see Rita B. Danjerous's personnel file now. *Please*. It's important.

Thank you.

Noah Memree
Principal

APPLETON ELEMENTARY SCHOOL

314 Apple Pie Avenue ⊙ Appleton, Illinois 61428

"We aim to grow with excellence and avoid
branching out unless absolutely necessary"

To: Noah Memree

From: Gladys Friday

Subject: RE: RE: RE: Important

Date: November 30

Dear Mr. Memree,

You're welcome. But I was thinking of the other magic words: *Summer. Vacation.*

You hired Ms. Danjerous on the last day of school, remember? It was right before the final bell. That's when I left for my well-deserved summer vacation. The last thing I reminded you to do was to check Rita's references. If you forgot to contact her previous employers, that would represent a serious lapse in judgment on your part. *Your* job could be on the line when Dewey A. Proove comes from the Illinois Department of Education to inspect our school paperwork.

Thank you.

Gladys Friday

Gladys Friday
Appleton Elementary School
Executive Administrative Assistant Extraordinaire

APPLETON ELEMENTARY SCHOOL

314 Apple Pie Avenue ◉ Appleton, Illinois 61428

**"We aim to grow with excellence and avoid
branching out unless absolutely necessary"**

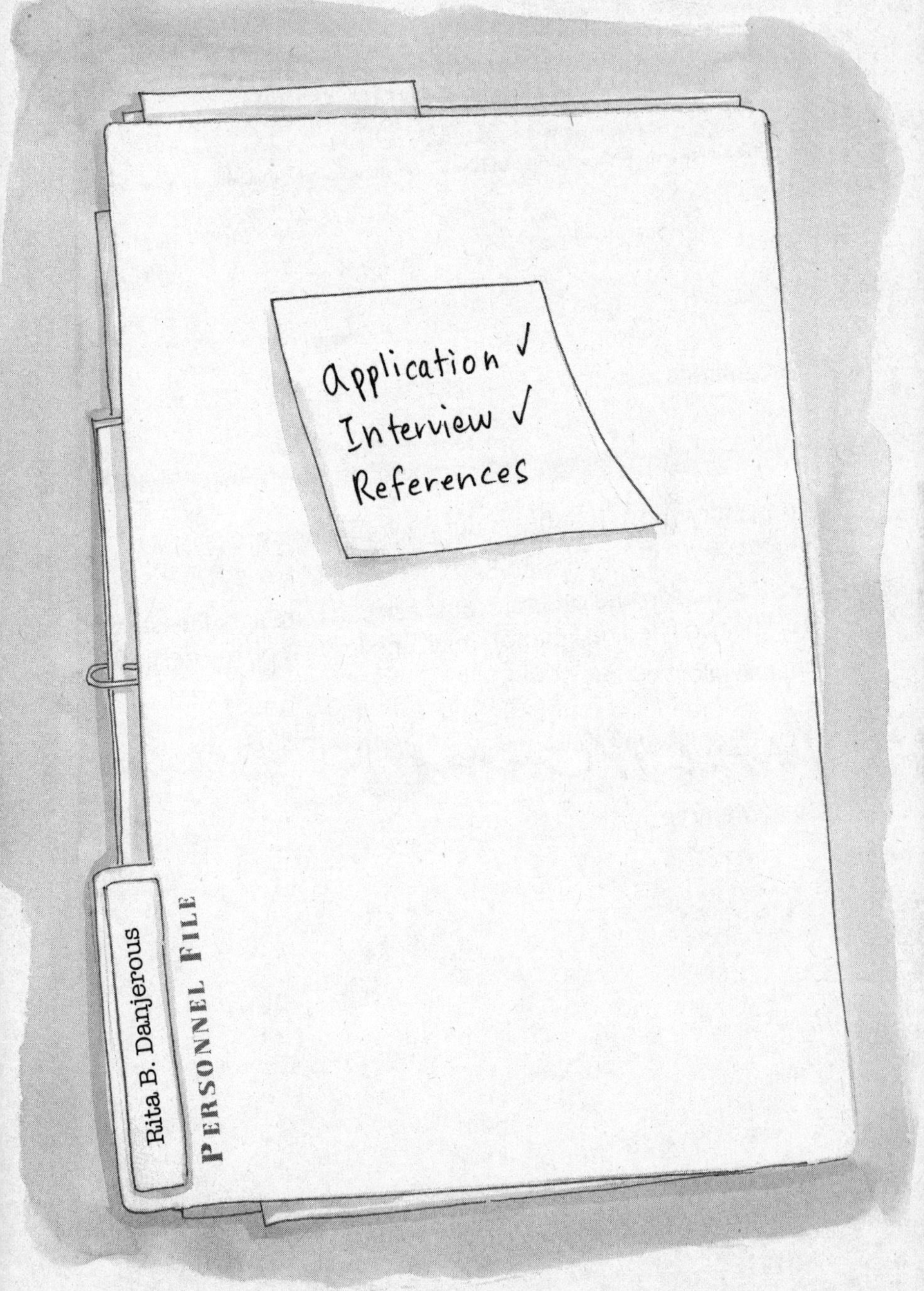
Application ✓
Interview ✓
References
Rita B. Danjerous
PERSONNEL FILE

December 1

Dear Ms. Danjerous,

Long story short: It appears during your hiring process, we neglected to cross all the t's and dot all the i's.

For this reason and others, I must ask you to resign. Please fill out the attached resignation form and leave it on my desk.

Thank you.

Noah Memree

Noah Memree

APPLETON ELEMENTARY SCHOOL

Resignation Form

Name of employee:
Position:
Reason for resignation:

Signature _____
Date_____

Rita B. Danjerous　　　　　　**Librarian & Bookworm**

If you've got a problem, I've got a book!

December 2

Dear Mr. Memree,

You seem like a decent man. I don't think you're particularly effective in your job, but I can work with people like you, mainly because I know how to work around people like you.

Ivana Beprawpa is a different story. She's a petty, greedy, narcissistic autocrat. I know she's behind all this, and I won't let her win. I *can't* let her win.

Mr. Memree, consider the children in this school. It is our responsibility as adults to show them bullies don't win. If I quit a job I love because of Ivana Beprawpa, it would send the wrong message to students. It would say if you're mean, loud, and not above telling lies or making threats, you can get your way, even if it's wrong. I might be a Danjerous woman, but I am not a threat to society. Ivana Beprawpa is.

This is a very long way of saying no, I will not voluntarily resign. If you want me to leave Appleton Elementary School, you'll have to fire me.

Sincerely,

Rita B. Danjerous

Rita B. Danjerous

APPLETON ELEMENTARY SCHOOL

314 Apple Pie Avenue ....Appleton, Illinois 61428

"We aim to grow with excellence and avoid branching out unless absolutely necessary"

Mr. Noah Memree
Principal

December 3

Dewey A. Proove
Illinois Department of Education
100 N. 1st Street
Springfield, Illinois 62777

Dear Mr. Proove,

Hello, sir. How are you? How are things at the Illinois Department of Education?

I wanted to drop a friendly note to say there is no hurry in visiting Appleton Elementary School for our inspection. In fact, if I were you, I'd put this school last on your list. We often have snow in December and our small-town snowplow can be quite sluggish.

May I suggest you consider postponing your visit to Appleton until spring? The month of May is quite lovely here. Just trying to be helpful.

See you soon—but not too soon, I hope.

Noah Memree

Noah Memree

IVANA BEPRAWPA

SCHOOL BOARD PRESIDENT
APPLETON SCHOOL DISTRICT
328 Baked Brie with Apples Avenue
Appleton, Illinois 61428

December 4

Dewey A. Proove
Illinois Department of Education
100 N. 1st Street
Springfield, Illinois 62777

Dear Mr. Proove,

Hello again! I'm so looking forward to your visit. I'm especially eager to hear your thoughts on our school librarian. She really *is* a big problem. I'm hoping you can help us find a way to let her go quickly and quietly.

If there's any chance you can come to Appleton sooner rather than later, please do. We're ready to welcome you with open arms! If you need accommodations in Appleton, I have a guest room I can offer for $150 per night. Cash payment preferred.

See you soon. The sooner the better!

Yours with impeccable manners and a comfy guest room,

Ivana Beprawpa

Ivana Beprawpa

DEWEY A. PROOVE

Chief Compliance Officer   **Illinois Dept. of Education**

100 N. 1st Street
Springfield, Illinois 62777

December 9

Noah Memree
Appleton Elementary School
314 Apple Pie Avenue
Appleton, Illinois 61428

Ivana Beprawpa
School Board President
328 Baked Brie with Apples Avenue
Appleton, Illinois 61428

Dear Mr. Memree and Ms. Beprawpa,

In reference to your letters:

The Illinois Department of Education has determined that an on-site visit to evaluate the management, staff, policies, procedures, and paperwork at Appleton Elementary School will be best achieved without advance warning.

In other words, my visit to your school will be a surprise.

Officially,

Dewey A. Proove

Dewey A. Proove

FIRST BANK OF APPLETON

Because Money Doesn't Grow on Trees

207 Apple Fritter Street
Appleton, Illinois 61428

Penny Counter
Loan Officer

December 11

Ivana Beprawpa
Owner, Beprawpa Attire
328 Baked Brie with Apples Avenue
Appleton, Illinois 61428

Dear Ms. Beprawpa,

On my way to work this morning, I saw several boys outside your store. I stopped to ask what was going on. They were standing in line to return their bow ties. They told me two boys are sewing custom-made ties, and that theirs are much "cooler" than yours.

This new development of children returning uniforms and demanding refunds makes me more concerned than ever about your ability to repay the money you owe this bank.

As of today, you owe:

$5,000 for the loan to produce campaign yard signs

$5,000 for the business loan to keep Beprawpa Attire afloat

$10,000 total due

I can give you one more extension, but that's it. If we don't receive full payment by December 21, we will have no option but to turn this matter over to a collection agency. Believe me, that won't be pretty or polite. You could end up in court.

Consider this your final warning. **We must receive full payment from you by December 21.** Or—and forgive me if this sounds rude or improper—else.

Sincerely and solemnly,

Penny Counter

Penny Counter

REID DURR

December 12

Ivana Beprawpa
Beprawpa Attire
328 Baked Brie with Apples Avenue
Appleton, Illinois 61428

Dear Ms. Beprawpa,

Hope the pickle sales are picking up! Hey, can you please send the money you owe me? Ms. Danjerous has gotten me so fired up about sewing, I want to buy my own sewing machine.

Thanks!

Reid Durr

Reid Durr

DURR'S ORCHARD

Highway PB at Apple Blossom Road
Appleton, Illinois 61428

>—i—<>—O—<>—i—<

ORDER & INVOICE

Date: October 12

Bill To:

Ivana Beprawpa
Beprawpa Attire
328 Baked Brie with Apples Ave.
Appleton, Illinois 61428

Ship To:

Same

Quantity	Description	Unit Price	Amount
10,000	Dill pickles	$.25	$2,500
		TOTAL	$2,500

PAYMENT OVERDUE

Payment due: 30 days

Please send payment to: Reid Durr
Highway PB at Apple Blossom Road
Appleton, Illinois 61428

THE DAILY APPLE

Bringing you all the juicy news, even when it's rotten to the core

316 Apple Pie Avenue
Appleton, Illinois 61428

Etta Toryal
Publisher & Editor

December 14

Ivana Beprawpa
Beprawpa Attire
328 Baked Brie with Apples Avenue
Appleton, Illinois 61428

Dear Ms. Beprawpa,

You've fallen behind in your ad payments. The current balance owed is $275.

I'd suggest taking care of this as soon as practical because a 5 percent late fee is added to all invoices 30 days past due.

Sincerely,

Etta Toryal

Etta Toryal

IVANA BEPRAWPA

SCHOOL BOARD PRESIDENT
APPLETON SCHOOL DISTRICT
328 Baked Brie with Apples Avenue
Appleton, Illinois 61428

December 15

Noah Memree
Appleton Elementary School
314 Apple Pie Avenue
Appleton, Illinois 61428

Dear Mr. Memree,

Your refusal to fire Rita B. Danjerous has caused me enormous personal and professional grief.

We have a school board meeting on Friday night. At the meeting, I plan to deal with this matter once and for all.

Are you with me in support of terminating Ms. Danjerous—or are you going to defend this woman who is polluting our town with her filthy books, corrupt morals, and complete lack of manners?

The future of Appleton looks to you, Mr. Memree. What will you do?

Ivana Beprawpa

Ivana Beprawpa

APPLETON ELEMENTARY SCHOOL

314 Apple Pie Avenue ....Appleton, Illinois 61428

"We aim to grow with excellence and avoid branching out unless absolutely necessary"

Mr. Noah Memree
Principal

December 16

Ivana Beprawpa
Appleton School Board
328 Baked Brie with Apples Avenue
Appleton, Illinois 61428

Dear Ms. Beprawpa,

You're right. Ms. Danjerous must go. Let's do it as quickly and quietly as possible.

Sincerely,

Noah Memree

Noah Memree

MEDIA RELEASE
For Immediate Release to All Appleton News Organizations

IMPORTANT MEETING OF
THE APPLETON SCHOOL BOARD

Contact: Ivana Beprawpa
Release date: December 17

(Appleton, IL) The Appleton School Board will meet on December 18 at 7 p.m. in the Appleton Elementary School cafeteria. On the agenda will be two issues of grave concern to the Appleton community:

> 1) a personnel matter which we should be able to conclude without too much discussion, and
>
> 2) a proposal to make pickles a required snack food for all Appleton Elementary students.

If you're interested in one or both issues, please plan to attend this meeting. Community input is neither requested nor encouraged, but your presence at these public meetings is always welcome, mainly because it is mandated by law.

Ms. Toryal,
Do you have an audio recorder we could take to this meeting? We want to catch every word.
Thanks!
Sarah May

APPLETON SCHOOL BOARD MEETING

Friday, December 18

Please sign in so we have a record of everyone in attendance.

Noah Menue

Penny Counter

Etta Toryal

IvanaBeprawpa

Rita B. Danjerous

Ceg Durr

Ben Thinken

Reid Durr

Gladys Fridays

May B Danjerous

Sarah Bellum

TRANSCRIPT

APPLETON SCHOOL BOARD MEETING

IVANA BEPRAWPA: Thank you for coming to tonight's meeting. I'll try to keep this brief. [Sound of throat clearing.] Oh, democracy. Shall I compare thee to an apple tree? Sometimes you require a gentle pruning. Other times you send out a wayward branch that needs a forceful whack. And sometimes, fair democracy, you produce an apple so rotten, it must be eliminated to save the rest of the crop.

NOAH MEMREE: If you're talking about a faculty member, we should discuss that in a closed-door session.

MAY B DANJEROUS: I'm pretty sure she's talking about my mom. I'd like to hear what she has to say.

SARAH BELLUM: Me, too.

IVANA BEPRAWPA: Good. Then I'll cut to the chase. It has come to my attention that Rita B. Danjerous is corrupting our school and town.

RITA B. DANJEROUS: Really? How exactly am I doing that?

IVANA BEPRAWPA: Oh, don't be coy. You've got the girls wearing fishnet stockings. The boys are sewing. And all the children are reading books from your depraved green dot collection.

BEN THINKEN: Which books do you object to, Ms. Beprawpa?

IVANA BEPRAWPA: I object to them all!

REID DURR: I didn't know you'd read the entire green dot collection.

IVANA BEPRAWPA: I don't need to read a book to know I don't like it. It's the idea of the books I object to. And it's not just her books. It's her background, too.

RITA B. DANJEROUS: What about my background?

IVANA BEPRAWPA: Yes, what about her background? I'm sure her prior employers must've provided some dirt, er, I mean, relevant information we can use against her. What did her references say, Mr. Memree?

NOAH MEMREE: Um, I don't have that information at my fingertips.

IVANA BEPRAWPA: Whatever. I know for a fact Ms. Danjerous is not from here.

MAY B DANJEROUS: Is it illegal to move from one place to another?

IVANA BEPRAWPA: No, but it's highly suspicious. It explains why she's not like us.

RITA B. DANJEROUS: In what way am I not like you?

IVANA BEPRAWPA: Well, for one thing, you're a single mother. Are you divorced?

SARAH BELLUM: Is it against the law to be divorced?

IVANA BEPRAWPA: No, but I don't approve of it. It's not good for children. Are you married, Ms. Danjerous?

RITA B. DANJEROUS: I'm not. Are you married?

IVANA BEPRAWPA: I am a respectable widow! My husband died twenty-seven years ago after a long and proper illness.

RITA B. DANJEROUS: My husband died four years ago after a terrible car accident.

GLADYS FRIDAY: Oh, Rita. We had no idea. I'm so sorry for your loss.

RITA B. DANJEROUS: Thanks. But do you know how I got through it? How my daughter and I both got through it?

NOAH MEMREE: Through what, Ms. Danjerous?

RITA B. DANJEROUS: The grief. The sadness. The feeling of, oh, what's the point of getting up in the morning and trying to live another day in a world that can be so unbearably sad? Do you know, Ivana?

IVANA BEPRAWPA: I don't.

RITA B. DANJEROUS: Then I'll tell you. The day after my husband's funeral, May and I crawled into my bed and we read. I started with biographies of strong women because I thought their stories would inspire me.

MAY B DANJEROUS: I read my old comic books.

RITA B. DANJEROUS: A few days later, we were still in bed. That's when May and I started reading together, alternating pages and then chapters. We used different voices for the various characters. Some days we wanted to read sad books. Other days we needed happy books.

MAY B DANJEROUS: We read mysteries, thrillers, love stories, ghost stories, graphic novels, even joke books with punch lines about zombies with snoring problems and worms that fart.

RITA B. DANJEROUS: *Books.* A word so small and humble, but I can say without a doubt that when I'd lost the will to live, books saved me.

MAY B DANJEROUS: They saved me, too.

RITA B. DANJEROUS: I truly believe books could save your school and your town if you would just give them a chance.

CY DURR [wiping away a tear]: Rita, that was beautiful. I hope you'll give love another chance. Give *me* a chance.

IVANA BEPRAWPA: Oh, would you shut up? Just shut up! This is neither the time nor the place for a romantic interlude. If we could simply fire this Danjerous woman once and for all, we could move forward with the second item on the agenda, which is the very sensible proposal that we put pickles on the school lunch menu and require that all elementary stu—

[ENTER DEWEY A. PROOVE]

DEWEY A. PROOVE: I don't think that's necessary.

GLADYS FRIDAY: Mr. Proove, is that you? I knew you'd arrive when we least expected it. How long have you been here?

DEWEY A. PROOVE: Long enough.

IVANA BEPRAWPA: Finally, Mr. Proove! You've come just in time to help us fire this woman who, as you can see, has turned our community upside down and caused unspeakable grief and aggravation.

DEWEY A. PROOVE: Actually, Ms. Beprawpa, I'm here to fire you.

[SOUND OF POLICE SIRENS IN THE DISTANCE]

THE DAILY APPLE

Bringing you all the juicy news, even when it's rotten to the core

Etta Toryal, Publisher & Editor   50 cents   Saturday, December 19

PICKLEGATE!

School Board President Arrested and Charged with Influence Peddling, Pickle Pushing

by Sarah Bellum and May B Danjerous

Ivana Beprawpa is apprehended by police.

After a dramatic school board meeting last night, Ivana Beprawpa was arrested and charged with using her position as Appleton School Board President for personal financial gain.

"I became aware of this situation when I received a letter from Ms. Beprawpa, urging me to buy her pickles," said Dewey A. Proove, chief compliance officer for the Illinois Department of Education. "She was using school board stationery to promote a personal fund-raiser, which is a clear violation of our conflict-of-interest policy."

"But the fifth-grade girls gave me that stationery!" Beprawpa said in her defense. "They told me in a note that we wouldn't want anyone to think I had a conflict of interest. I have it in writing!"

The original letter did not use the word *we*. It said, "You wouldn't want anyone to think you have a conflict of interest between your clothing business and your school board responsibilities." But Beprawpa clearly did.

In addition to improperly peddling pickles, Beprawpa also tried to enforce a school uniform policy that benefited her clothing store, Beprawpa Attire. The shop is now closed. (See story on next page.)

Ivana Beprawpa spent the night in the Appleton Jail. She will face a jury trial next year.

Memree Going; Beprawpa Bound for Bankruptcy

by Sarah Bellum and May B Danjerous

Noah Memree will step down as principal of Appleton Elementary School, effective at the end of the month.

"It has come to my attention that I am not as effective as I would like to be," said Memree, who plans to reevaluate his career path and work on his memory and management skills. A new principal has not been named.

Meanwhile, as Ivana Beprawpa was led away by Appleton police last night, she told the crowd gathered at the school board meeting that she will file for bankruptcy.

"You can forget about collecting any money from me," she hollered. "I don't have a thin dime to my name!"

When asked if this meant she would also close her store, Beprawpa said, "Of course it means I'm closing my store! The brats in this town don't know how to dress. I tried to help them look like proper young ladies and gentlemen, but did they listen to me? No!"

How does she feel about the orange jumpsuit she'll have to wear in jail?

"Huh?" she replied. "Is that true? Orange jumpsuit? Seriously?"

Ivana Beprawpa then said a very bad word and fainted.

Meet Dewey A. Proove

by Sarah Bellum and May B Danjerous

We know Dewey A. Proove isn't an Appleton resident, but we wanted to learn more about him. So we met him at the Apple Cart Café for a quick interview after the school board meeting.

Sarah: Thanks for agreeing to talk to us.

May: Thanks for coming to Appleton, too.

Dewey: My pleasure.

Sarah: What did you think when you arrived at the school board meeting?

Dewey: Well, the first thing I noticed was Ivana Beprawpa's abysmal manners and her remarkable lack of decorum. But what struck me most was how smart and savvy you kids are. Thank goodness Appleton's fifth graders were keeping a close eye on Ivana Beprawpa. You figured out how she was using her job in public service to secretly make money for herself.

May: Luckily, she wasn't very successful.

Sarah: Or very secretive.

Dewey: Exactly. Now there's something I'd like to clear up. May, is your middle name really B?

May: Yes.

Dewey: No punctuation after it?

Proove approves of Appleton's fifth graders.

May: Just B, like the letter.

Dewey: Well, if that's the case, your paperwork is officially complete and approved. You are the twentieth student enrolled at Appleton Elementary. The school will remain open.

Highway PB at Apple Blossom Rd.
Appleton, Illinois 61428

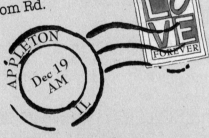

APPLETON
IL
Dec 19
AM

Rita B. Danjerous
Appleton Elementary School
314 Apple Pie Avenue
Appleton, Illinois 61428

DURR'S ORCHARD

Delicious Apples   Homemade Cider   Select Fruits & Veggies

Highway PB at Apple Blossom Road
Appleton, Illinois 61428

Cyrus "Cy" Durr
Founder and Owner

December 19

Rita B. Danjerous
Appleton Elementary School
314 Apple Pie Avenue
Appleton, Illinois 61428

Dear Rita,

What a week! You must feel exhausted and exhilarated.
I can't help smiling when I think it was my pickled
cucumbers that helped to bring down the reign of Ivana
Beprawpa.

Reid asked me to tell you the fifth-grade research team
learned that Pilgrims may very well have served pickled cabbages and turnips at the first Thanksgiving, but
probably not pickled cucumbers. Pickling, according
to your researchers, is a traditional way of preserving
food to keep it from spoiling. But even pickles couldn't
hide the rot of Ivana's regime.

Speaking of Reid: I'm so proud of the courage he's
shown this year. Now it's time for me to be as brave as
my son.

Would you be interested in coming over for dinner
this weekend? I've mastered the recipes for Fantastic
Fajitas, Tantalizing Tostadas, and Chocolate-Lover's

Cheesecake. (They're on pages 79, 94, and 136 of the cookbook Reid brought home from your library.)

Reid and May can join us for dinner, or we can dine alone. Your choice. I'd just like to spend time getting to know you better. How in the world did you become you?

I await your reply.

December 21

Cy Durr
Durr's Orchard
Highway PB at Apple Blossom Road
Appleton, Illinois 61428

Dear Cy,

I'm flattered by your kind words and generous invitation, but I'm going to pass. May and I will spend the weekend packing.

I'll be honest with you: The only reason I got the job at Appleton Elementary was because Mr. Memree forgot to check my references. If he had, he'd have discovered that I've been fired from every job I've ever held. Something about me just seems to get under people's skin. Wherever I go, I get caught up in these crusades, whether it's creating a green dot collection of books that are a little edgy, or encouraging girls to wear whatever clothes they like, or protecting boys who want to hang out together and sew. These things are important to me, but I end up complicating a lot of people's lives, including my own.

Don't get me wrong. It's satisfying (and fun!) to expose the shenanigans of people like Ivana Beprawpa. But let's face it, Cy. There are a lot of Ivana Beprawpas in the world. I don't understand how people like that end up in charge, but they often do. People like me usually get fired or, if not, we get so discouraged or exhausted or just plain broke that we end up leaving.

So that's what I'm doing. I'm going to fill out the official resignation form and put it on Mr. Memree's desk. He won't find it until he comes in to pack up his things next week. By then, May and I will be off on our next adventure.

I'm glad you think we were victorious. Maybe we were. I knew I couldn't resign while Ivana Beprawpa was still in power. But now that she's out of office, I think it's time for me to go, too.

I can't thank you enough for your kindness over these past few months. I'll never eat another apple without remembering your sweet face and lovely orchard.

Take care,

Rita B. Danjerous

P.S. How did I become me? Not sure I know how, but I'm pretty sure I know when. It was after many years of trying to be everyone but me.

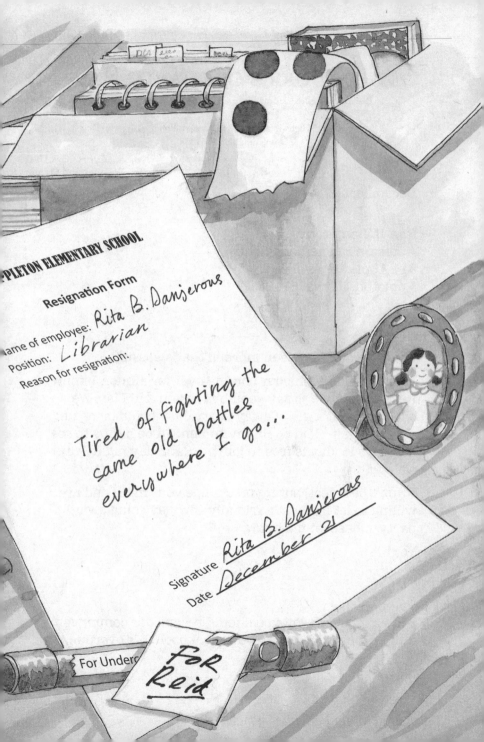

DURR'S ORCHARD

Delicious Apples   Homemade Cider   Select Fruits & Veggies

Highway PB at Apple Blossom Road
Appleton, Illinois 61428

Cyrus "Cy" Durr
Founder and Owner

December 22

Rita B. Danjerous
Appleton Elementary School
314 Apple Pie Avenue
Appleton, Illinois 61428

Dear Rita,

Now I admire you even more, if that's possible.

I wish you'd reconsider coming over for dinner. I know Reid would love to say good-bye to you and May. We could make it a going-away party. May could bring her friend Sarah. Reid could invite Ben. I'd be happy to see if Gladys Friday is free to join us. Saturday night? Six o'clock?

I won't be a pest, but if you change your mind and are willing to let me host a friendly, low-key going-away party, please let me know.

Your fan,

P.S. Another reason you should reconsider coming for dinner: I need to return your cookbook. It's overdue.

APPLETON ELEMENTARY SCHOOL LIBRARY

December 23

Cy Durr
Durr's Orchard
Highway PB at Apple Blossom Road
Appleton, Illinois 61428

Dear Cy,

You know the way to a librarian's heart: returning overdue books!

May and I will be there on Saturday night at six o'clock.

Rita

P.S. Thanks again for being so nice.

MENU

Danjerous Going-Away Party

Saturday, December 26

Six o'clock

May B Delicious Appetizers

Rita & Weepa Fajitas

Fit-to-Be-Tried Tostadas

and the

Danjerously Decadent Dessert Bar,

featuring

Gladys Chocolate Cheesecake

CITY OF APPLETON POLICE DEPARTMENT
Report of Possible Criminal Activity

DAY & DATE: Saturday, December 26

LOCATION: Appleton Elementary School

DESCRIPTION OF ACTIVITY: While driving past Appleton Elementary School shortly after 10 p.m., I noticed lights on in the main office. I pulled into the parking lot (no siren) and entered the school with my city-issued keys.

I found four 5th graders inside the school. They admitted to unlawfully entering the principal's office with the help of Gladys Friday. (Gladys has keys to everything.)

The kids were finishing up a project that involved putting little green stickers all over a resignation form. The girls said they'd explain everything in tomorrow's paper.

Report submitted by:

Cory Peel

Cory Peel, Chief of Police
Appleton Police Department

THE DAILY APPLE

Bringing you all the juicy news, even when it's rotten to the core

Etta Toryal, Publisher & Editor $1.50   Sunday, December 27

Students Caught Green-Handed!

by Sarah Bellum and May B Danjerous

Fifth-grade students and Friday found in principal's office.

What do you do when a beloved school librarian submits her resignation? If you're a fifth grader at Appleton Elementary School, you break into school and cover that resignation form with hundreds of little green dot stickers so that Principal Noah Memree can't read it.

"It was Ben's brilliant idea," said Reid Durr, referring to his pal, Ben Thinken. "He suggested we use Ms. Danjerous's green dots to make her resignation unreadable."

The four students who participated in last night's caper couldn't have pulled it off without the help of former Executive Administrative Assistant Extraordinaire Gladys Friday. At the request of Ben and Reid, Friday drove them, along with Sarah Bellum and May B Danjerous, to school after a festive going-away party at Durr's Orchard.

"I told Rita and Cy I was taking the kids out for ice cream," said Friday. "But instead I drove them directly to school."

Appleton Police Chief Cory Peel didn't issue a ticket or make an arrest of Friday or the children. "It's not officially breaking and entering if Gladys had the keys. But I gave them all a warning and called their parents. Now I'm wondering how these kids intend to keep this a secret from Noah Memree."

"Oh, don't worry about that," said Friday. "Mr. Memree never remembers to read the newspaper."

Rita B. Danjerous, who found out about the scheme from Police Chief Peel, said she was at first shocked by the students' sneakiness, but then touched by the sentiment behind it.

"Maybe Appleton is where I belong after all," Danjerous said, adding that she and her daughter now plan to stay in town until the end of the school year.

Gladys Friday Glad She's Principal

by Sarah Bellum

The new Appleton School Board, comprised of Penny Counter and Cy Durr, along with members of the fifth-grade class, met on Friday night. The board chose Gladys Friday to serve as Appleton Elementary School principal beginning in January, when the new semester starts.

"If it's okay with everyone," said Friday, "the first thing I'd like to do is pick a new school motto. Maybe something about how we believe in branching out? Or, maybe we could be Appleton Elementary, Home of the Bookworms. I'm open to suggestions!"

Friday appears undaunted by the prospect of taking over from Noah Memree. Asked who she'll hire to be her secretary, Friday waved her hand through the air. "Pfft, I'm glad to do both jobs. I've been doing it for years anyway."

The good news for Friday and others is that calls have been pouring in from families outside the area, planning to move to Appleton in the near future. Unlike a few months ago, when the school was in danger of closing because of low enrollment, Appleton Elementary now has a waiting list of students hoping to enroll.

"People are hearing about Picklegate and how our fifth graders uncovered the scandal," said Friday. "Now every parent within 500 miles wants their kids to come to our school."

Fifth Graders Publish True Crime Book

by Etta Toryal

Rita B. Danjerous says the newest book in the Appleton Elementary library might be her favorite.

"It was written and illustrated by the fifth-grade class," said Danjerous. "How could I not love it?"

The book, *Don't Judge a Crook by Its Cover*, is a nonfiction account of the recent goings-on at Appleton Elementary.

"The title is a play on words," explained Sarah Bellum. "Everyone knows the saying, 'Don't judge a book by its cover.' Our book is basically the story of how a local crook named Ivana Beprawpa tried to cover her crimes by pretending to care about manners, morals, and education. The truth is, the only thing she cared about was making money for herself."

The book was written by Sarah Bellum and May B Danjerous, with Reid Durr and Ben Thinken serving as illustrators. Asked if the classmates plan to publish any future books, the foursome looked at each other and laughed.

"Maybe!" said Ben Thinken. "But let's hope nothing this scandalous ever happens again in Appleton."

Students donate book to school library.

FOREVER

APPLETON
Dec 31
AM
IL

Dewey A. Proove
Illinois Department of Education
100 N. 1st Street
Springfield, Illinois 62777

May B Danjerous
1322 Apple Tart Place
Appleton, Illinois 61428

December 31

Dewey A. Proove
Illinois Department of Education
100 N. 1st Street
Springfield, Illinois 62777

Dear Mr. Proove,

Thanks again for visiting Appleton!

I've been thinking about our recent conversation at the Apple Cart Café. Remember when I told you that my middle name is the letter B with no period after it? Well, that's true, but I should've told you why my parents gave me that name.

When I started kindergarten, my mom told me my middle name would be a reminder that I can B anything I want to B, and nothing can stop me. It sounds like a little thing, but when you're feeling sad or lonely or just scared about being the new kid in school, it's nice to have a built-in reminder that all I have to B is me.

Happy New Year to you and yours!

Sincerely,

May B Danjerous

May B Danjerous

P.S. I hope you'll come back to Appleton. Something tells me next year is going to be even more interesting!

ACKNOWLEDGMENTS

When you begin your publishing career, nobody tells you how many friends you'll meet through books. Over the years, our young readers have become our pen pals. Our editors feel like special sisters. And the teachers, principals, and PTO parents we've met at schools around the country have welcomed us like long-lost friends.

But it's the librarians who have surprised us the most. Who knew there existed such a sly, smart, subversive band of bookworms devoted to spreading mischief and mayhem (we mean that in the best way!) in schools and public libraries on a daily basis? This book is our tribute to them. We cannot end without thanking a few librarians by name:

Thank you, Cathy Evans, for introducing us to the concept of a green dot collection; to Alison Smithwick for schooling us on when, why, and how books are challenged; to Uma Hiremath for her warmth and wisdom, and to everyone at the Ames Free Library in North Easton, Massachusetts, for their summer hospitality; to Lex Anne Seifert, librarian-at-large, for always making us think and laugh; to Joel Shoemaker for telling us we weren't, in fact, retired when we thought we were; to Cynthia Cooksey for showing us how fun sewing machines could be in a library; to Ed Carson for the endless coffee; to Denise Lough Nicholas for loving baseball as much as books; to April Rosso for convincing us we could learn PowerPoint (ha!); to booklover Kerri Kunkel, who isn't a librarian but we love her just the same; to our brother, James Klise, who *is* a librarian, a top-shelf YA author, and always the first person to read our manuscripts.

And thank *you*, whoever you are, for reading these words right now. Spending time together in these pages connects us to you and to the world. At the risk of sounding corny, the process of putting words and pictures together to tell a story makes our hearts feel full, true, and wonderfully *ripe*. As William Shakespeare wrote more than four hundred years ago: *"Ripeness is all."*

—Kate and Sarah

Looking for more great characters in
stories filled with fun and adventure,
written by Kate Klise
and illustrated by M. Sarah Klise?

Read on for a sneak peek at

BOOK 1
Three-Ring Rascals

THE
SHOW
MUST GO ON!

❧ CHAPTER ONE ☙

If you're ever walking down a dusty road and see a sign that looks like this, **STOP** and look closely.

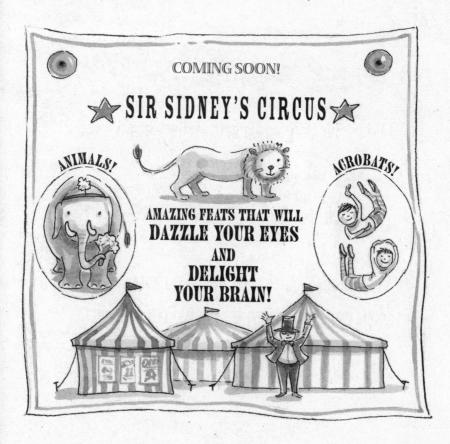

COMING SOON!

⭐ **SIR SIDNEY'S CIRCUS** ⭐

ANIMALS!

ACROBATS!

AMAZING FEATS THAT WILL
DAZZLE YOUR EYES
AND
**DELIGHT
YOUR BRAIN!**

For years, Sir Sidney and his circus traveled to towns and cities around the world. Were audiences always amazed?

Were they dazzled and delighted?

Did people gasp and giggle and wave and wiggle?

Were children admitted **FREE OF CHARGE** and given all the hot popcorn they could possibly eat?

"And did we clean up after every show by eating all the spilled popcorn?"

I'm Bert.

You bet!

I'm Gert.

Aw! Aw!

And that's Old Coal the crow.

But during all those years of travel, did Sir Sidney grow old and tired? He most certainly did. He needed someone to help him.

So not long ago, Sir Sidney placed an ad in the newspaper.

Well, you can imagine the response! Hundreds of men and women stood in line for hours for a chance to talk to Sir Sidney.

But Sir Sidney met a man at the very end of the line who claimed to be PERFECT for the job.

My name is Barnabas Brambles. I have a degree in lion taming from the University of Piccadilly Circus in London, England.

Will Barnabas Brambles get the job?

Will Sir Sidney's Circus still dazzle and delight?

Will children and mice still get all the popcorn they can eat?

Read on to find out in

Three-Ring Rascals, Book 1:

THE
SHOW
MUST GO ON!

Kate Klise is the award-winning author of more than 30 books for young readers, many of which are illustrated by her sister, M. Sarah Klise. On her way to becoming an author, Kate Klise worked as a baby-sitter, waitress, ice-skating instructor, and rosebush pruner. She was also a journalist and spent 15 years reporting for *People* magazine. When she's not working on a new book, she enjoys traveling around the country, sharing her best writing tips and tricks with aspiring authors of all ages.

M. Sarah Klise has always had a fondness for creating colorful book reports, which began in elementary school with yarn-bound volumes on states and countries. In college, she enjoyed writing heavily illustrated letters home to her mother. Years later, she still does variations of all that when she illustrates books for young readers. She also teaches art classes in Berkeley, California.